GW00730677

A Precious Moment

J. Eileen

Copyright © 2023 J. Eileen
All rights reserved
First Edition

Fulton Books
Meadville, PA

Published by Fulton Books 2023

This book is a work of fiction. Any references to historical, real people, or real locales are used fictitiously. Other names, characters, places, addresses, and incidents are products of the author's imagination, and any resemblance to actual events or locales or persons, living or dead, is entirely coincidental.

ISBN 979-8-88505-969-5 (hardcover)
ISBN 979-8-88505-968-8 (digital)

Printed in the United States of America

Prologue

Dave and Katy begin a wonderful life together with Chester, a Maine coon cat, and Samson, a cockatoo, residing at the three-story yellow Victorian house located in the country outside of the town, Sweetwater, Oklahoma, where several mysteries develop.

Samson, the cockatoo, is out of his cage every morning, but the door on the cage is still latched shut. An open cracker box is also found on the kitchen counter every morning with a cracker missing.

On the other side of the open bookcase entrance under the hidden oak staircase, Father Williamson notices a door.

Chester admires a new friend at the Garden and Landscape Store.

Dave and Katy's first sledding party in January and Valentine's Day celebration in February do not end well.

A big surprise is coming for Dave, Katy, Chester, and Samson.

Will Dave and Katy be able to solve the mystery of how Samson, the cockatoo, gets out of his cage and why a cracker box is lying open on the kitchen counter with a cracker missing every morning?

What lurks behind the door under the hidden oak staircase on the other side of the open bookcase entrance?

Who is the new friend Chester is admiring at the Garden and Landscape Store?

Why doesn't Dave and Katy's first sledding party and Valentine's Day celebration end well?

What will the surprise be for Dave, Katy, Chester, and Samson?

A new year begins!

Chapter 1

A new year has begun for Dave, Katy, Chester, and Samson.

Chester had just awakened and extended his front claws to sharpen them on his scratch post, which stood in the corner of the music room. He walked quietly to the kitchen and ate some of his dry gentle cat food and drank some water. *That was really tasty. That should be enough for me until Katy or Dave can fill my bowl with egg and cheese bits with white sauce. I am ready for the first day of the year*, thought Chester as he walked quietly to the sitting room. The grandfather clock struck six o'clock in the morning. Chester carefully pressed the television remote control. *My favorite cartoon is on. Oh, look! A new batch of catnip toys for me to play with. I can roll on them, toss them in the air, and catch them. What fun!* thought Chester.

Suddenly, a red flashing light started blinking around the sitting room. Chester looked up toward his cat condo. There in the window was a large sign with blinking lights. *Oh, what a surprise. Dave and Katy must have hung the sign on the window when they got home from their New Year's Eve party. It says, "Happy New Year." How thoughtful of them to wish me a happy New Year*, thought Chester as he continued playing with his catnip toys and watching cartoons on television.

A screeching sound was heard coming from the music room. *That is my buddy, Samson. He wants out of his cage. I must hurry before he wakes Dave and Katy. That cockatoo wants to watch cartoons with me!* thought Chester as he scampered down the hall to the music room.

"I am coming! I am coming! Don't worry, ole buddy. I will get this door on your cage open. Stay calm and quiet. We don't want to wake Dave and Katy," said Chester as he raised the latch of the door on the cage up and waited for Samson to walk out. Samson was nodding his

head in an affirmative manner, thinking that would speed Chester up in unlatching the door to his cage. Chester carefully closed the door on the cage and slid the latch downward back in place.

"You're my friend! You're my friend! Got me out! Got me out! Free again! Free again! Thank you, friend! Thank you, friend!" squawked Samson loudly.

"Shshsh! Stay quiet, Samson! We need to keep it a secret that I can open the door to your cage! Follow me!" said Chester as they walked together back to the sitting room. Samson walked behind Chester, making the clickety-clack, clickety-clack sound with his feet on the hardwood floor. *"Fly up and sit on your perch,"* said Chester.

"Don't mind if I do! Don't mind if I do!" said Samson as he spread out his white wings and flew to the tall, sturdy wooden perch. He fluffed his feathers and began to observe the program on television. A new program was starting. The narrator announced, "David and Goliath!" Samson instantly spread out his wings and started flying around the sitting room. He screeched loudly when he heard the name Goliath.

"Stop! Stop! Samson, please stop! You are going to wake everyone up! I am taking cover. I will hide in this large circular tube of my cat condo. Hopefully, no one will see me," Chester said as he hurriedly crawled inside.

"What is going on?" Katy asked as she sat up in bed with a startled look on her face.

"I will go find out," Dave said as he put his slippers on.

"I am coming with you," Katy said.

As Dave and Katy were walking through the hall, Mother and Father Williamson were walking down the spiral stairway. As everyone walked into the sitting room, all was quiet. Samson was standing on his wooden perch with his back to the television, and Chester was peering out of the circular tube of his cat condo, looking very scared.

Just then the boy on the television said loudly, "Goliath! Goliath! There is the giant Goliath!"

Samson immediately spread out his wings and took flight through the air and screeched loudly as he flew around the sitting room. Dave walked up to the television and turned it off. Samson

settled down and flew back to his wooden perch. Chester was still hidden in his circular tube, hoping he had turned invisible so no one would see him. "A program called 'David and G-O-L-I-A-T-H' was on television," Dave said.

"Samson definitely does not like that name," Katy said. "Who let Samson out of his cage?" Katy asked.

"I have no idea. It wasn't me," Dave said.

"We just got up," Father Williamson said.

"Let's go take a look at the cage," Dave suggested.

They walked to the music room and looked down at the cage.

"I can't believe this!" Katy exclaimed.

"The hook is still latched on the door of the cage. I suppose Samson can disappear and appear in and out of his cage," Mother Williamson remarked.

"I don't know," Dave said, laughing quietly. "It will be a mystery until we get it solved. What a way to start the new year!"

"Let's have breakfast," Katy said.

"I will put the coffee on," Mother Williamson said.

As Katy was placing the scrambled eggs into a bowl, she remembered Chester had not been fed. She walked over to Chester's white cupboard to get his clean bowls and noticed there was a bowl sitting in front of his white cupboard on the floor that had a small amount of dry food sitting in it. "Chester has already been fed," Katy said. "Did someone get up early and feed Chester?" Katy asked.

"Not me," Dave said.

"Like I said, we just got up when we heard Samson screeching," Father Williamson said.

"Oh, goody!" Dave exclaimed. "Another mystery to solve to start the new year off."

"I will give Chester fresh water just in case our mystery visitor didn't do that," Katy said as she placed a bowl of fresh water and a bowl of egg and cheese bits in white sauce in front of Chester's white cupboard.

"Perhaps, Katy, Chester didn't eat all his food last night," Mother Williamson said.

"He has never done that before, but there is always a first time," Katy said.

Wow! That was close. I need to watch what program is on television when Samson is in the sitting room. I sure am glad I know how to use the television remote, thought Chester as he crawled out of his circular tube and walked to the kitchen to eat his breakfast.

"What are the plans today?" Father Williamson asked.

"I would like to take all the Christmas decorations down inside the house," Dave said. "The decorations on the front porch could be taken down and placed in the basement to dry. Katy would like the wreaths hanging on the double doors left for a while though."

"If we all work together, it shouldn't take long," Katy said as she poured fresh-squeezed orange juice into a glass.

"Where do you want to store everything?" Mother Williamson asked.

"I thought we could store the artificial tree and decorations throughout the house in the room on the other side of the bookcase opening beside the stairway that leads to the third story," Katy said. "Then I could still redo the floor and paint the ceiling and walls on the third story. Please don't block the stairway leading up to the third story."

"We also need to make sure Samson is in his cage or an enclosed room," Dave suggested. "I don't want him flying through the bookcase opening to the third-story room. It may be difficult to get Samson out of there."

"We will keep the glass-paned double doors closed when we open the bookcase," Katy said.

"That is a great idea," Dave said.

By noon, all the decorations were taken down and stored, except for the two wreaths on the double doors of the front porch and the artificial tree and lights of the gazebo in the back of the house. Dave didn't want to put the artificial tree and lights on the gazebo away while they were still covered with snow and very wet. Everyone agreed that waiting till spring to complete that task was a fantastic idea.

Katy and Mother Williamson were in the kitchen, preparing lunch. Father Williamson and Dave had just finished setting the artificial Christmas tree that sat in the hall on the other side of the bookcase entrance across from the open staircase.

"Dave, what is behind this door under this oak stairway?" Father Williamson asked.

"I have no idea," Dave answered with a puzzled look on his face. "It is probably a closet or storage area." Dave walked over to the side of the oak stairway. "I will open the door and see what is lurking behind it," Dave said in a mysterious voice jokingly. The door made a creaking sound as Dave opened it. The bottom of the door slowly dragged on the floor.

"That is what it is, a small closet," Father Williamson said, peering inside.

"It is a very small space," Dave said. "Not big enough to store anything. The floor seems hollow underneath. Listen as I walk on it."

"You are right. It does sound hollow," Father Williamson responded curiously.

"Shine your light down toward the floor," Dave said.

"Look!" Father Williamson exclaimed. "There is a black handle embedded in the wood floor, and at the side are black hinges."

"Let me lift it up and take a look," Dave said. He took hold of the black handle and pulled. The entire floor raised up inside the closet. "There are steps leading down," Dave said. "I wonder where these steps lead to."

"Won't know until one of us goes down and finds out," Father Williamson said.

"I will go down first, Dad, and see where they lead," Dave said. "I don't know how sturdy these steps are, and I don't want you to get hurt. First, I need to get the large spotlight from our bedroom." The steps creaked loudly as Dave carefully walked down the steep wooden stairway.

"See anything, Dave?" Father Williamson asked.

"I have reached the bottom," Dave answered. "There is another door. It is padlocked shut. I don't see a key anywhere. I have no idea where the key would be."

"We will probably have to break the padlock to see what is on the other side of the door," Father Williamson suggested.

"I am coming back up," Dave said as he carefully walked up the creaky steps. "We need to let Katy and Mother know about this. Katy might know where the key is."

"Good idea," Father Williamson replied. "It is time for lunch anyway. I just heard Katy call us for lunch."

Dave walked up the steps and dropped the floor back in place and closed the door.

Ham sandwiches, potato chips, and individual dessert dishes filled with layers of red, yellow, orange and green Jello were on the table for all to enjoy. "That was a delicious lunch," Dave said. "I really worked up an appetite putting the Christmas decorations away."

"We have another surprise," Mother Williamson said.

Katy opened the oven door and pulled out a pan. She filled four dishes and carried them to the table on a tray.

"Bread pudding!" Father Williamson exclaimed. "I haven't had that for a long time."

"I have never had Katy's bread pudding," Dave said as he spooned a small amount of bread pudding from his dish and took a bite. "This is wonderful, Katy. Make this again!" Dave exclaimed.

"It is exactly the way your mother makes it," Father Williamson commented.

"Dad, shall I tell Katy and Mother what we found?" Dave said.

"I think we should," Father Williamson said.

They told them about the door under the oak stairway that had a steep stairway leading to a door that was padlocked.

"Have you been in that room behind the padlocked door?" Dave asked.

"This is the first time I have heard of this!" Katy exclaimed with a shocked look on her face. "I want to see this," she said anxiously as she got up from the kitchen table and quickly walked to the music room. Dave pushed the lever up inside the bookcase, and it opened. "I can't believe we never noticed this door before," Katy said as she pulled the door open under the oak staircase.

"Let me lift the floor up," Dave said.

"What is at the bottom of the steps?" Katy asked as she peered down below.

"I walked down the steps, and there is another door that is padlocked," Dave answered. "I don't have any idea where the key would be."

"There is a key hanging on a hook in that closet off the kitchen where I keep my cleaning items, broom, and vacuum," Katy said. "I had no idea what the key was for but kept it hanging on the hook just in case we figured out what door it might unlock. I will go get it."

It wasn't long. Katy was back, dangling a key from a chain in front of Dave. "I don't know if this key will unlock the door, but it is worth a try," Katy said anxiously.

"I will go down and see if the key unlocks the padlock," Dave said. "All of you stay up here." Dave carefully walked down the narrow, steep, creaky steps and placed the key at the bottom of the padlock. He turned the key to the right. "Bingo! The key opened the padlock!" Dave shouted excitedly.

"Dave, be careful," Katy said in a concerned voice. "You have no idea what is on the other side of that door."

"I will come down with you," Father Williamson said as he slowly made his way down the narrow, steep stairway.

"John, be careful," Mother Williamson said.

Dave pushed the door open. As it opened, it creaked and dragged on the concrete floor. Father Williamson followed Dave, holding the spotlight so it would beam brightly toward their pathway ahead as they walked into a large empty room.

"It is really cold down here," Dave said.

"What did you find?" Katy asked.

"It might have been used as a cellar to keep food during the winter months," Father Williamson said. "Families would butcher their own meat and keep it in caves through the long winter months so they would have food to eat."

They flashed the spotlight around the room and gasped.

"There is another door!" Dave exclaimed.

"Mother and I are coming down!" Katy shouted. "I don't want anything to happen to you and Father."

"No, Katy, stay up there," Dave said. "If something should happen, you will be able to call for help." Dave slowly opened the door. "It is a tunnel!" Dave exclaimed in a loud voice with excitement. "An underground tunnel with concrete walls, ceiling, and floor. I have no idea where it leads to!" Dave exclaimed.

"Dave Middleton, you and Father get back up here right now!" Katy said in a stern, demanding voice. "You should not go in that tunnel by yourself. We need to get Sheriff Jesse and Deputy James to look at this."

"You are probably right," Dave said. "I will close the door to the tunnel and padlock the door at the bottom of the steps before coming up." After everything was closed and locked up, Dave went to the sitting room to call Sheriff Jesse.

"Sheriff Jesse, how may I help you?"

"Hi, Sheriff Jesse. This is Dave Middleton. I was wanting to know if you and Deputy James could drive out today. There is something we would like to show you."

"Sure, Deputy James and I can be there at three o'clock this afternoon," Sheriff Jesse said.

"Great, see you then," Dave said.

Later, the bell rang on the front porch.

"Happy New Year!" Sheriff Jesse and Deputy James said together.

"What is going on?" Sheriff Jesse asked.

"We found another area in the house that leads to an underground tunnel," Dave answered. "We didn't feel comfortable walking through the tunnel without you seeing it."

"Let's take a look at it," Sheriff Jesse said in a curious voice.

Sheriff Jesse, Deputy James, Dave, and Father Williamson started down the narrow, steep stairway that made a creaky sound as they walked. Dave unlocked the padlock and opened the door. They then walked into the large empty room and opened the door that led to the underground tunnel.

"Oh my!" Sheriff Jesse exclaimed. "Who would have imagined this house had an underground tunnel."

"Would you have any idea where it would lead to?" Dave asked.

"This is an old house, and years ago, houses like this had underground tunnels that led to another house to keep their family and friends from being captured," Sheriff Jesse said. "I am going to call Ralph, who is head of an investigating team in Springville, Oklahoma. They will accompany us as we walk through this tunnel to see where it leads to."

"It might lead to a dead end," Deputy James said.

"Don't let anyone know about this," Sheriff Jesse said. "I will get back in touch with you sometime this week. Close everything up and padlock the door. Don't do anything until you hear from me."

"Okay, thanks, Sheriff Jesse and Deputy James," Dave said, shaking their hands.

"We will be waiting to hear from you," Katy said.

"Your father and I need to be on our way," Mother Williamson said.

"Keep us informed on the underground tunnel," Father Williamson said.

"We definitely will," Katy said. "Here are your clean clothes, and thank you for coming and helping us during your stay."

"Let me carry your luggage to the car," Dave said.

"If you need us for anything else, just give us a call," Father Williamson said as he shook Dave's hand and gave Katy a kiss on her cheek.

"Yes, be sure and do that," Mother Williamson said, kissing Dave and Katy on the cheek.

"Take care and have a safe drive home," Dave and Katy said as they waved goodbye.

Chapter 2

"Katy, I need to go to work," Dave said. "Come on, Samson, time to go to work." Samson flew through the air and stood on Dave's left shoulder.

"Samson work! Samson work!" Samson repeated several times as he nodded his head forward and backward.

"Scott and I are going to take the Christmas decorations down today. I will see you this evening. Be sure to call me if you hear anything from Sheriff Jesse and Deputy James. I want to be here when the investigation team comes to look at that underground tunnel."

"I will let you know when they call," Katy said, giving Dave a big hug.

"Have a great day!" Dave exclaimed.

"You, too, honey," Katy said.

*****

"Hi, Dave," Scott said. "Peggy and I came in yesterday and put all the Christmas decorations away. I am ready to start inventory."

"That is great!" Dave exclaimed. "Thank you!"

"Do you think Katy can help us with inventory this week?" Scott asked.

"That is a great idea," Dave answered. "It sure would go a lot faster. I will give her a call right now."

Dave dialed the number on the phone.

"Hello, the Middletons, this is Katy speaking."

"Hi, Katy! How is everything going?" Dave asked.

"It is really lonely in this great big house," Katy said. "To be truthful, I am bored."

"I have a suggestion to take care of that loneliness and boredom," said Dave.

"What would that be?" Katy asked.

"Scott and I sure could use some help with the inventory at the store this week. Would you be interested in coming in to help starting tomorrow?" Dave asked.

"It would be great to come and help with the inventory at the store," Katy said anxiously. "Chester and I don't go back to the library to read a book and help with refreshments and crafts until next Wednesday afternoon."

"Great!" Dave exclaimed. "See you this evening when I get home from work. We will talk about what I need help with after our supper."

"I will be looking for you. Goodbye!" Katy said as she hung up the phone.

Chester was just finishing his beef and gravy as Dave walked through the back door of the enclosed porch with Samson on his shoulder.

"Samson, your supper is in your bowl beside Chester," Katy said. Katy placed a platter of meat loaves on the table.

"Something smells good," Dave said. "Meat loaf, baked potatoes, corn, and peas!" Dave exclaimed. "This will surely hit the spot after a hard day at work." After dinner, Dave helped Katy clear the table and placed the dishes and silverware in the dishwasher.

"Let's go to the sitting room," Katy suggested. "I want you to tell me what you need help with at the store."

Samson and Chester were standing on the top shelf of the cat condo, looking out the window, watching the large snowflakes fall.

"That is the first time I saw Samson on the top shelf of the cat condo," Dave remarked.

"Yes, Chester and Samson have become true friends," Katy said as she sat beside Dave in a wingback recliner chair.

"I need help with inventory and taking care of customers when they come in," Dave said.

"Sounds good to me," Katy said. "If a customer comes in, I will assist them while you and Scott continue with the inventory."

"We should be able to complete the inventory by the end of the week," Dave said. "I will even take Chester and you to lunch at Sammy's Sugar Shack," Dave said.

"That's an offer I can't refuse," Katy said, chuckling. "Would you like a cup of hot cocoa before going to bed?" Katy asked.

"Sure, that would satisfy my craving for something sweet," Dave said.

Chapter 3

Katy had just finished cleaning up the breakfast dishes and sweeping the kitchen floor.

"Honey, Samson and I will be leaving for the Garden and Landscape Store," Dave said as he put his coat on.

"Chester and I will be right behind you, Dave," Katy said.

"It sure will be good to get the inventory finished," Dave said.

"Yes, another thing to cross off the need-to-do list," Katy said, giving him a hug and kiss.

"Okay, see you both at the store," Dave said as he walked out the door with Samson on his shoulder.

"Samson work! Samson work!" Samson said as Dave opened the truck door.

"Chester, ride," Katy said. Chester ran to his white cupboard in the kitchen and grabbed his collar from the peg. Katy put the collar around Chester's neck and snapped his black leash on his collar, locked the house door, and off they went to the car. Chester sat in the front passenger seat.

Look at all the white snow glisten and sparkle! The trees are covered heavily with white snow too. What a beautiful sight. There is always something new to see when I go for a ride, thought Chester.

"Chester, we will be going to the Garden and Landscape Store every day this week," Katy said as she drove down the country road to the town of Sweetwater, Oklahoma. "I don't want you to do your disappearing and reappearing act you sometimes do when I call for you to come." Chester meowed softly as he continued watching the beautiful sights through the car window.

"We are here!" exclaimed Katy as she and Chester walked into the Garden and Landscape Store. *Oh boy! Where is my buddy, Samson?*

thought Chester as he scurried to the room where the guinea pigs, hamsters, birds, and aquariums of fish were.

"Hey there, Chester, good buddy, good friend. I am over here! I am over here!" Samson said loudly when he saw Chester enter the room.

"Hi, Samson!" Chester said as he looked up and saw Samson standing on his wooden perch, watching the hamsters go around on their wheel inside of their cage. *"Samson, you better be careful watching that wheel go around and round and round. You will get dizzy and fall off your wooden perch,"* warned Chester.

"Me! Not me!" Samson exclaimed loudly. "I am a cockatoo and a smart one at that. Nothing can make me fall."

As the wheel in the hamster cage continued going around, Samson began swaying side by side. Samson then leaned forward and then backward and *thump!* Samson had fallen off his wooden perch and was lying on the floor.

Oh no! My friend! My pal! My buddy! Wake up, Samson! Please wake up! thought Chester. Samson did not make any movement. He just lay quietly on the floor. *I need to get help fast!* thought Chester as he quickly ran to the room where Katy, Dave, and Scott were counting clay pots on a shelf. Chester meowed loudly, did a circular twirl, put his right front paw up, and looked toward the room where Samson was lying. Chester continued to meow loudly, trying to get their attention.

"Look, Dave!" Katy exclaimed. "Chester is doing that same thing with his front paw when he wanted us to follow him to Dark Woods on Halloween night last year."

"We better go see what he wants," Dave said.

Dave, Scott, and Katy followed Chester to the room where Samson was lying on the floor.

"Oh no! Something is wrong with Samson," Katy said.

"Don't touch him," Dave immediately said. "Let me call the vet. We need to find out what to do. We don't want to hurt him."

"Is he still alive?" Katy asked.

"I hope so," Dave answered.

Dave dialed the veterinarian clinic in Springville, Oklahoma.

"Springville Veterinarian Clinic, this is Tammy. How may I help you?"

"Hi, Tammy, this is Dave Middleton. Is Doc Adams available?" Dave asked.

"He is on a call at a farm," Tammy said. "I can transfer you to his mobile phone if you like," Tammy offered.

"Yes, that would be great. Thank you," Dave said.

"This is Doc Adams. What can I do for you?" Doc Adams asked.

"Hi, Doc, this is Dave Middleton."

"Hi, Dave, hope all is okay," Doc Adams said.

"My cockatoo is lying on the floor," Dave said. "I don't know if he is alive. I didn't want to move him and cause any other damage."

"I will be there in fifteen minutes," Doc Adams said in a concerned voice. "I am at a farm just outside Sweetwater."

"Okay, we will be looking for you," Dave said. "We are at the Garden and Landscape Store."

Doc Adams walked into the store, and Dave showed him where Samson was lying.

"What do we have here?" Doc Adams said in a soft, soothing voice. "Nothing seems to be broken." Doc Adams gently rolled Samson to his side. He pressed his fingers tenderly in areas of his body and listened to his heart with his stethoscope and opened each eyelid. "He might have had the wind taken out of him when he fell to the floor. Where do you think he was before he fell?" Doc Adams asked.

"He usually stands on his wooden perch and watches the hamsters run on their wheel," Dave said.

"That might have made him dizzy, and he fell off his wooden perch," Doc Adams said. "His heart is beating normally. He is probably in shock. Be sure he has fresh water and a small amount of food. Let me know tomorrow how he is doing."

"Okay, thanks, Doc," Dave said.

"Yes, thank you, Doc Adams, for coming so quickly," Katy said. "We will keep a close watch on him."

"How long have you had him?" Doc Adams asked.

"We got him the week before New Year's Day," Dave said. "The driver who delivers our items to the store was trying to find a home for him. A cockatoo needs attention, or they become very stressed. Katy's father took him in, and he always has someone to be with and talk to. If he isn't at the store, he is at our home. He gets along great with Chester. They have become real pals. Just don't say the name G-O-L-I-A-T-H. He goes frantic if we say that name."

"Keep him calm and away from stress," Doc Adams said.

Samson was very quiet the rest of the day. Katy and Chester left the store at four o'clock in the afternoon. Dave came, walking into the house with Samson on his shoulder at half-past five. He placed Samson on his wooden perch in the sitting room. Samson closed his eyes and went to sleep.

Samson, please be okay. You are my friend, my pal, my buddy. I have so much to show you once the snow disappears. I want all the animals and birds in Dark Woods to meet you. I know Trudie Butterfly will be absolutely amazed at how handsome you are, thought Chester as Samson continued to sleep. Dave placed Samson inside his cage before going to bed. Chester slept outside Samson's cage. *"I am here for you, buddy. If you need anything, just say my name,"* Chester said in a sympathetic kitty voice. Chester closed his eyes and went to sleep.

Chapter 4

"Chester! Chester! Squawk! Squawk!" Samson shouted loudly. Chester woke up with a startled look on his face.

"What is it, Samson? What do you need?" Chester asked, looking at Samson with his half-open eyes.

"Samson free! Samson free!" Samson said.

"Okay, buddy, but you have to be careful. You had a bad fall yesterday," Chester said as he unlatched the hook and opened the door to the cage.

"Cracker! Cracker!" squawked Samson as his feet went clickety-clack, clickety-clack on the hardwood floor toward the kitchen.

"Wait here. I will get the crackers out of the cupboard," Chester said as he jumped on the counter and started opening cupboard doors. *Now where does Katy keep those crackers? Ah, here they are!* thought Chester as he pushed the box of crackers out of the cupboard onto the counter. Chester extracted his claws on his front paws and tore an opening at the top of one of the rectangle packages inside the cracker box. He removed one cracker from the package and slid it over the counter and let it drop to the floor. Samson immediately walked to the cracker and started eating it.

"Mmmm! Good cracker!" Samson said.

"Samson, I have some advice for you. To keep from getting dizzy watching the hamsters run on their spinning wheel, you need to turn around so you have your back toward them. When you hear the wheel stops spinning, you can turn around and watch them again. If the wheel begins to spin again, turn around so your back is facing the spinning wheel. I don't want you to fall again. Come on, Samson. Let's go to the sitting room and rest a bit. I am still tired," Chester said. Down the hall they went. Samson followed Chester making loud clickity click

sounds with his feet on the hardwood floor in the hall. *"You probably aren't strong enough to fly to your wooden perch, and I can't put you on it. You may sit in my cat bed if you like,"* Chester said. Samson wobbled over and stepped in Chester's cat bed, fluffed his feathers outward, then folded them back in close to his body, and went to sleep. Chester climbed to the top of his cat condo and went to sleep too.

Dave and Katy had awakened.

"I wonder how Samson is doing," Katy said.

"Go check on him," Dave said as he put his robe and slippers on. "I will be out in a minute."

"Dave, Samson is not in his cage!" Katy exclaimed. "The hook to the door of his cage is still latched."

"What!" exclaimed Dave. "I have to see this!" he said as he walked out of the bedroom. "Do you know where he is?" Dave asked.

"No," Katy said with a worried look on her face.

"Let's go check the kitchen," Dave said.

"Did you get up and eat crackers last night, Dave?" Katy asked as she walked into the kitchen, seeing the box of crackers on the counter and a rectangle package was open at the top with one cracker missing.

"No, I slept all night, darling," Dave answered with a shocked look on his face and giving a chuckle.

"I slept all night, too, darling," Katy said.

"Let's check the sitting room," Dave suggested.

As they walked into the sitting room, they couldn't believe what they saw. Samson was standing in the cat bed, and Chester was curled up beside him, sleeping.

"I don't know what happened and who did what, but no harm was done," Dave said.

"They definitely are true friends, and they sure look innocent," Katy said with a pleasing smile.

"Yes, it sure looks that way," Dave said.

"I will put on a pot of coffee and make breakfast while you take a shower and get dressed for work," Katy said.

Katy had just finished flipping the last pancake on the griddle.

"Good morning, Chester and Samson!" Katy said. "You are probably hungry." She placed a bowl of bird seeds and a bowl of eggs with cheese bits and white sauce in front of the white cupboard. "Here is a bowl of fresh cool water for each of you," Katy said.

"Samson cracker! Samson cracker!" Samson said, tapping his feet loudly on the kitchen floor.

"It looks like you already had a cracker, Samson," Katy answered, shaking her index finger at him. "I sure would like to know how you escaped from your cage and the door is still latched. Now you are able to find the crackers in the cupboard. How do you do that, Samson?" Katy asked.

"Don't tell her, buddy. Dave and Katy can never find out that I am able to let you out of your cage and now give you a cracker," whispered Chester.

Samson immediately started to eat his bird seed and did not say another word about wanting a cracker.

"How is it going?" Dave asked.

"Fine, Samson wants a cracker, but I told him he had to eat his bird seed first," Katy said.

"He told you he wanted a cracker," Dave said.

"Yes!" Katy answered.

"That is a good sign," Dave said. "He is walking and talking. Have you seen him fly?" Dave asked.

"No," Katy answered. "He just follows Chester making those clickety-clack sounds with his feet as he walks on the tile floor in the kitchen and the hardwood floor in the hall."

Dave just grinned.

"I was hoping I could get Samson to talk when I asked how he escapes from his cage and now has the knowledge in getting a cracker out of the cracker box," Katy said. "But I had no luck in getting Samson to talk. It was as if Chester told Samson to be quiet because when I asked Samson about this, Chester immediately looked at Samson, and Samson immediately put his head down and started eating his bird seed."

Dave started laughing, and Katy instantly got very perturbed with him. "Detective Katy is at work once again looking for the culprit who lets Samson out of his cage and retrieves a box of crackers from the cupboard, which shows one cracker is missing," Dave said, chuckling. "I don't know why you let all this bother you. There is no harm done."

"You have to agree, Dave. It is rather strange to see Samson out of his cage, and the latch is still hooked shut on the cage door, and there is only one cracker missing," Katy answered as she placed a plate of three large pancakes on the table in front of Dave. "It is a mystery, and I want it solved."

"Samson and I are going to work," Dave said as he took one last sip of his coffee. "See you and Chester at the store."

"Yes, we will be leaving after I have the breakfast dishes cleaned up," Katy answered. "How are you going to keep Samson from watching the hamsters spin on their wheel?" Katy asked.

"I don't know," Dave answered. "Do you have any suggestions?" Dave asked.

"Maybe Samson won't watch the wheel spin anymore," Katy said. "Chester won't watch a paint can shake in the machine at the hardware store and knows when to stop watching something that goes around and round like the electric train in the toy store window," Katy said.

"We will soon find out," Dave said. "I am relieved Samson is feeling better."

"Me too. See you shortly," Katy said.

*****

"Chester, ride," Katy said, holding the black leash. Chester came running with his collar in his mouth and did a fancy twirl and a chirpy meow. "What has gotten into you, Chester? You seem to be extra excited to go for a ride today. Do you miss Samson?" asked Katy as she fastened the collar around Chester's neck. Chester instantly did another twirl and meowed two times. "Let's get going," Katy said. "Samson and Dave are waiting for us."

Katy and Chester walked into the store. Dave was standing at the cash register. "Shshshsh! Follow me," Dave said in a quiet voice.

"You have to see it to believe it." They walked into the room where the hamsters were running speedily on their wheels. Samson was standing on his wooden perch with his back facing the wheel. When the wheel stopped turning, Samson would turn around and watch the animals and birds in their cages. "You were right, Katy," Dave said. "He knows what made him dizzy."

"He definitely is an intelligent bird," Katy said. "Just like Chester is an intelligent cat."

"Are we going to get some inventory done today?" Scott asked.

"Yes, we better get started," Dave and Katy said together as they walked to the garden and yard tool area of the store.

"Don't forget to call Doc Adams," Katy said. "He wanted to know how Samson was doing today."

"I will do that right now," Dave answered.

"Don't forget to tell him how Samson is keeping from getting dizzy," Katy said, chuckling.

"Thank you for reminding me," Dave said as he walked to the phone in his office.

Later, the inventory at the Garden and Landscape Store was completed. Peggy, Scott's girlfriend, came to help after she closed her Interior Decorating Store in Springville, Oklahoma, at five o'clock in the afternoon. Dave and Scott would now know what needed to be ordered for spring. Dave, Katy, Chester, and Samson arrived at their home shortly after nine o'clock at night, and they were very tired. They fed Chester and Samson their supper and then enjoyed their fish sandwiches with tartar sauce, curly fries, cabbage salad, and chocolate shakes that Dave had ordered at Sammy's Sugar Shack. Dave placed Samson in his cage.

It sure has been a long week. I must lay close to my pal, Samson. He might want a cracker during the night, thought Chester as he curled up in his cat bed beside the harp.

"I would like to watch the news before going to bed," Dave said.

"I will stay and watch it with you," Katy said. "Maybe there will be some news about a cracker thief in other homes."

"Katy, you can't be serious, are you?" Dave asked. "I mean, really!" Dave exclaimed.

"I am telling you, Dave, we have no idea who or what lurks inside this house during the night," Katy said in a serious voice.

"If someone was lurking inside our house, Samson would be squawking and yelling for help, and Chester would be going wild like he did when the intruders broke into our home while we were on our honeymoon," Dave said.

"I got it!" Katy exclaimed.

"Got what?" Dave asked loudly.

"I will ask Sheriff Jesse and Deputy James to come to our home and place a bright light over Samson and ask him questions," Katy said.

"You don't mean to interrogate Samson, do you?" Dave asked.

"Yes, that is what it is called, interrogate Samson!" Katy exclaimed. "I know it will work. Let me see, what kind of questions could be asked?" Katy asked. "I got it!" she exclaimed.

"Got what?" Dave asked loudly.

"The questions that should be asked to Samson," Katy said.

"Tell me all about it, Katy," Dave said.

"Okay, I will tell you how it should be done," Katy said.

"Okay, bird, who gives you the cracker from the cracker box in Dave and Katy's kitchen? Speak up, bird! Start talking, or there won't be any more crackers for you in the days to come. I know there is someone giving you a cracker and also letting you out of your cage. Confess, bird, who is the mysterious visitor causing all this chaos in Dave and Katy's home? All right, you made your choice, bird. No more crackers for you for one year. And a padlock will be placed on your cage. We will see if that mysterious visitor can unlock a padlock."

"I am going to bed," Dave said, shaking his head left to right. "We will talk about this tomorrow morning."

"Okay!" Katy exclaimed as she followed Dave to the bedroom.

Chapter 5

"Katy, what do you have planned for today?" Dave asked as he walked into the kitchen.

"Some cleaning, laundry, the usual weekend duties before Sunday," Katy answered quietly.

Chester, with Samson following behind him, walked into the kitchen. Their breakfast was in bowls in front of the white cupboard.

"Samson, you may eat your breakfast beside Chester, but you cannot eat Chester's food. The same goes for you, Chester," Katy said in a stern voice.

Katy doesn't seem to be in a happy mood. She must have gotten up on the wrong side of the bed, thought Chester as he gobbled down his egg and cheese bits in white sauce.

"This should be interesting to watch!" exclaimed Dave.

"It doesn't take Chester long to eat his food," Katy said. "I know Chester isn't going to like bird seed, and I rather doubt if Samson will take a liking to egg and cheese bits in a white sauce."

"You are probably right," Dave said, giving a grin.

"Since this is my Saturday off, I am going to shovel more snow, get the fireplaces started, and take it easy," Dave said. "It has been a busy week doing inventory."

"It has been a busy week for me, too, Dave Middleton!" Katy exclaimed with a disgusted look on her face. "As you recall, I helped with inventory too!"

"I am sorry, Katy, I should be offering to help you with the work inside the house," Dave said apologetically. "We will do the housework and laundry together. That way, it will get done faster. I don't know what I was thinking," Dave said, placing his arms around her waist.

"Thank you, Dave," Katy said with a smile. "You are such a wonderful, understanding husband."

Dave vacuumed the floors, polished the hardwood floor in the hall and the steps of the spiral stairway, mopped the tile floor in the kitchen, emptied the dishwasher, and did some light dusting while Katy cleaned the bathrooms and did the laundry. Dave helped Katy make the bed in the guest bedroom upstairs and the bed in their bedroom. By noon, they were finished and exhausted.

"What would you like for lunch, Dave?" Katy asked.

"Let's just have something light like sliced Colby cheese and some of that summer sausage with crackers," Dave answered. "We can go to the sitting room and sit in our recliners and enjoy a movie."

"Sounds good to me," Katy answered. "I will never pass up an offer like that."

As Dave and Katy walked into the sitting room, Samson was on his wooden perch, and Chester was curled up in his cat bed.

"Look, Dave, Samson must be able to fly again," Katy said. "He is standing on his wooden perch," she said with amazement.

"I see that," Dave said as he stoked the logs in the fireplace.

"I sure am glad he is feeling better," Katy said.

"Me too," Dave said.

Dave and Katy fell asleep. They woke up at three o'clock in the afternoon and noticed that Samson and Chester were no longer in the sitting room.

"I wonder where those two have gone off to," Katy said.

"I suppose we better go investigate," Dave said. "Who knows what they have gotten themselves into."

Dave and Katy walked to the kitchen, and the cracker box lay open on the counter.

"Looks like our mysterious visitor has been here again," Katy said.

"Let's keep searching," Dave suggested.

They walked through the open glass-paned oak doors to the music room. Chester was in his cat bed by the harp, sleeping soundly, and Samson was in his cage with the door latched shut.

"I can't believe this," Katy said. "Now Samson is in his cage, and the door to the cage is still latched. How does that cockatoo do that?" Katy asked.

"I have no idea," Dave answered. "I am going to shovel some snow before it gets too dark. A bowl of that homemade chili will sure taste good when I am finished," Dave said, winking his eye.

"I will make some grilled cheese sandwiches to go with it," Katy said.

Dave and Katy were sitting at the kitchen counter, eating their chili and grilled cheese sandwiches.

"Katy, you aren't serious about having Sheriff Jesse and Deputy James involved in this mysterious caper of Samson out of his cage and the door is still latched and a cracker missing from the cracker box, are you?" Dave asked.

"No, I was just having some fun," Katy said. "You have to agree. It would be interesting if Samson would give in and talk while Sheriff Jesse and Deputy James interrogated him."

"It also could make Samson very stressed, and he could become extremely ill," Dave said. "I don't know how I would explain it to the vet, Doc Adams."

"I agree. Like I said, I was just having some fun and wanted to see how you would respond," Katy said, giving a grin. "I would never want to stress Samson in any way and make him ill. Like you said, Dave, no harm has been done."

"Let me help you clean up these dishes," Dave said.

"Thank you, Dave. You are such a sweetheart," Katy said, giving him a kiss on the cheek.

Chapter 6

As the week passed by, a large amount of snow fell. By Friday, Sweetwater, Oklahoma, had gotten six and a half inches of snow.

"Dave, are we still planning to attend the sledding party tomorrow afternoon?" Katy asked.

"Yes, I am planning on it," Dave said. "I haven't missed one yet, and this will be your first time. Farmer Brown has the largest, longest hill that is perfect for all kinds of sleds to slide down. He also has an old one-room country schoolhouse that is heated by an old woodstove so the visitors can go inside and warm themselves with a cup of hot cocoa or apple cider. Everyone from Sweetwater will be there, and they are welcome to bring their relatives and friends from other towns if they like. It is always held on the last Saturday in January. You are going to love it!"

"Do you have a sled?" Katy asked.

"Yes, I have a long toboggan and a regular wood sled with steel runners on the bottom," Dave said. "They both work great on a snowy hill. The sleds are hanging in the storage room of the Garden and Landscape Store. I will bring them home today after work."

"What do we do with Samson?" Katy asked.

"See if your parents would want to come and stay the weekend," Dave suggested.

"Fantastic idea!" Katy exclaimed. "I will call them now," she said as she quickly walked to the sitting room to dial the phone number.

"Hello, the Williamsons!"

"Hi, Mother, this is Katy!"

"Is everything all right, dear?" Mother Williamson asked.

"Oh yes, everything is great," Katy said. "We got all the inventory done at the store. Samson had a little fall from his wooden perch while watching the hamsters go around on their wheel. He is doing fine."

"I am glad about that," Mother Williamson said.

"I have a favor to ask," Katy said. "I do hope it isn't too short of a notice."

"Yes, what is it?" Mother Williamson asked.

"The town of Sweetwater always has a big sledding party in the afternoon on the last Saturday in January," Katy said. "Dave and I would really like to attend, but we need someone to stay with Samson. Would you and Father like to come and stay for the weekend or longer?" Katy asked.

"I would love to," Mother Williamson answered. "Let me ask your father." Then she asked, "John, Dave and Katy want us to watch Samson, their cockatoo, while they go sledding tomorrow afternoon. What do you think?" Mother Williamson asked.

"I'm all for it!" Father Williamson exclaimed in a grumpy voice. "Do both of us good to get out of here! No need to be in a hurry getting home either. We can go to church with them on Sunday and head home toward the end of the week. I am beginning to get cabin fever staying in this house."

"Katy, your father is very anxious to come," Mother Williamson said. "I will start packing our bags, and we should be there before noon tomorrow."

"Oh, thank you, Mother, and thank Father too," Katy said. "It will be good to see you both. I know Dave is looking forward to it. It was his idea to ask if you could come."

"We are looking forward to it too," Mother Williamson said. "See you tomorrow."

"Yes, we will be watching for you," Katy said. "Dave and I love you both."

"Your father and I love you more," Mother Williamson said, giving a chuckle.

As Katy hung the phone up, it rang again. "The Middletons, this is Katy."

"Hi, Katy, this is Sheriff Jesse. Is Dave close by?" Sheriff Jesse asked. "I tried the Garden and Landscape Store, and there was no answer."

"Dave is running late this morning," Katy said. "I will go get him."

"Hi, Sheriff Jesse, how is everything going?" Dave asked.

"I got that investigation team lined up to walk through that underground tunnel. Would Monday at ten o'clock in the morning be all right for them to come?" Sheriff Jesse asked. "Deputy James and I will be with them also."

"Yes, that would be great," Dave said. "See you Monday at ten o'clock."

"If something should come up that we can't make it, I will let you know," Sheriff Jesse said.

"Katy and I will do the same if there's a conflict on our behalf," Dave said. "Katy, keep Monday open," Dave said as he hung up the phone. "Sheriff Jesse, Deputy James, and the investigation team are coming Monday at ten o'clock in the morning to walk through the underground tunnel," Dave said.

"Great, Mother and Father Williamson will be here," Katy said. "I am sure they are looking forward to finding out where that underground tunnel leads to and what it was used for," Katy said.

"Remember, Katy, we need to keep this quiet to everyone at the sledding party tomorrow afternoon and at church Sunday," Dave said.

"My lips are sealed," Katy said.

"Okay, I have to go to work," Dave said.

"I am going to make something scrumptious for Mother and Father to enjoy while they watch Samson tomorrow afternoon," Katy said.

Chapter 7

"Dave! Dave! Wake up! It's Saturday! Today is our first sledding party together!" Katy said excitingly as she tossed a soft fluffy pillow toward Dave's head.

"Ohhhh, I am so tired," Dave said in a sleepy voice. "Just a few more minutes of rest, please."

"I'll make coffee and waffles," Katy said.

"That sounds absolutely delicious," Dave said as he rolled over and fell out of bed.

"Are you all right?" Katy asked, looking over the side of the bed, giving a slight giggle.

"Yes, I am just really tired," Dave said.

"You sleep, and I will let you know when breakfast is ready," Katy said.

As Katy was busy squeezing the juice from the oranges and preparing the waffles, she heard Samson walking through the hall, making the clickety-clack sound with his feet. She knew Chester would be strolling in the kitchen ahead of Samson.

"Here you go, Chester and Samson," Katy said. "Breakfast is served. I need to finish making these waffles. I have a brilliant idea!" Katy exclaimed. "I will serve Dave breakfast in bed."

She got the bed tray from the cupboard and placed a white linen cloth over it. A plate with two waffles and a metal lid over the plate to keep the waffles warm was placed on the tray. A glass of ice-cold fresh-squeezed orange juice, a small pitcher of hot bubbly pure maple syrup, a small dish of butter, a mug with steaming hot coffee, and a napkin with a fork, knife, and spoon inside were placed on the tray also. Off she went, carrying the tray to the bedroom.

"Surprise! It's breakfast time, Dave!" Katy said.

"What a surprise, breakfast in bed!" Dave exclaimed. "I have never had breakfast in bed."

"Now you have," Katy said. "Eat up, my darling husband!" "You need your strength. We have a sledding party to go to this afternoon." Katy adjusted the pillows so Dave would be comfy sitting up. She placed the tray across Dave's legs.

"This is delicious, Katy," Dave said as he ate the last piece of his waffle.

"Mother and Father will be here before noon," Katy said.

"I will clean up the kitchen while you take a shower."

"I see it snowed again," Dave remarked. "I will shovel the walks and carry more firewood in the house to keep the fire burning so your parents will stay warm."

"Sounds like a plan," Katy said as she picked up the bed tray.

"Is Chester going to the sledding party?" Dave asked.

"I gave it some thought, and I think it would be best if he stays here with Samson," Katy answered. "When Mother and Father arrive, I will tell you about Chester's first sledding party. He was not a happy kitty."

The bell on the front porch rang.

"Mother, Father, come in out of the cold," Katy said. "Let me have your coats and hats. Dave, would you carry their luggage up to their room?" Katy asked.

"I will be happy to do that," Dave said.

"Come into the sitting room and get warm by the fire," Katy said. "I will make hot cocoa for you. Be back in a jiffy!" Katy exclaimed.

"We ate a small lunch at Sammy's Sugar Shack in Sweetwater before coming here," Mother Williamson said.

"Are you taking Chester to the sledding party?" Father Williamson asked.

"Dave and I have been thinking about that," Katy said. "Chester went to a sledding party with our church youth group when we resided at the apartment in Oklahoma City. Wasn't the best experience for Chester. He had a great time sliding down the hill but walking back up really wore him out. I have pictures. Would you like to see them?" asked Katy.

"Sure!" said Father and Mother Williamson together.

"You are right. He does not look like a happy kitty," Father Williamson said.

"I think Chester would be happier staying with Samson and his grammy and grampy," Mother Williamson said.

"I agree," Dave said.

"I made a homemade chicken and vegetable noodle soup," Katy said. "It is in the refrigerator. It will take a few minutes to heat it up. There is sliced cheese and bread if you want grilled cheese sandwiches with your soup. I also made a pan of brownies and chocolate chip cookies. Help yourself to anything."

"Make yourself at home," Dave said. "Our home is your home."

"Katy, we better get our warm clothes on if we are going to that sledding party," Dave said.

"Okay, it won't take me long to get ready," Katy answered. "I am going to wear my insulated tights and wooly socks and corduroy slacks with a heavy, bulky pullover sweater, along with my winter coat, stocking cap, scarf, mittens, and snow boots."

"You should stay warm wearing all that," Mother Williamson said.

"What about you, Dave?" Father Williamson asked.

"I am going to wear my insulated long johns, slacks, flannel shirt with a pullover sweater over it and put on my battery-operated heated socks, snow boots, gloves, winter coat, stocking cap, and scarf," Dave said.

"Do you happen to have another pair of battery-operated heated socks?" Katy asked.

"I sure do. I will go get them," Dave said.

"I must say, you both have made good choices to stay warm at that sledding party," Mother Williamson said.

The sledding party was a huge success. Many people of Sweetwater, Oklahoma, invited family and friends from other towns to attend. Farmer Brown's old one-room country schoolhouse was toasty warm while everyone talked among each other and enjoyed the hot cocoa, apple cider, coffee, cookies, and bars. The one-room country schoolhouse even had indoor restrooms. As people entered

the school building, there was an enclosed girl's restroom on the right side and an enclosed boy's restroom on the left side. They didn't have running water and the commodes were unable to be flushed like the commodes in homes. Farmer Brown made sure both restrooms were clean and had liquid soap in a bottle, along with a large jug of water with a spigot and plenty of paper towels so anyone who used the restroom could wash their hands.

"This sure takes the cold chill of the outdoor air away," Dave said as he took a sip of his hot cocoa.

"It was so nice to see our friends again," Katy said. "The winter months can bring on cabin fever to so many because they don't want to get out or can't get out."

"That won't be happening to us," Dave said. "There is plenty to do at the Garden and Landscape Store. You have Wednesday afternoons to read stories to the children at the Sweetwater Public Library."

"Mother and Father are only three hours away," Katy said. "I am sure they will be wanting to come to get away now and then too."

"It is great having them come and spend time with us. I wouldn't have it any other way, Katy," Dave said.

Chapter 8

The following morning, Dave woke up coughing heavily. "Katy, I am not feeling well," Dave said.

"You are running a fever!" exclaimed Katy as she placed her hand on Dave's forehead. "Let me take your temperature. It is 100.1 degrees. Put your robe and slippers on and come sit by the fire in the sitting room. I will make you a cup of hot tea with honey to help soothe your throat," Katy said.

"I don't think I will be able to attend church services today," Dave said.

"No one is attending church today," Katy said softly. "You don't need to catch something else along with that cough."

"Good morning. What is going on?" Father Williamson asked.

"Dave has a temperature and a cough," Katy answered. "If Mother and you are afraid of becoming ill, you probably should be on your way home."

"We will be fine, Katy," Mother Williamson said as she walked into the sitting room.

"We will keep the fire going and help all we can so Dave will soon feel better," Father Williamson said.

Dave didn't have much of an appetite. Katy heated up the homemade chicken and vegetable noodle soup she had made yesterday. She also made her famous ice cream malts. Katy's ice cream malts were the best. Her secret was using pure vanilla bean ice cream. To make a strawberry malt, she would stir in strawberry Crush soda through the vanilla bean ice cream. The chocolate malts consisted of vanilla bean ice cream, chocolate syrup, and a splash of fat-free white milk. The vanilla malt was made of vanilla bean ice cream and a splash of fat-free white milk.

"Dave, would you like me to call Scott to let him know you won't be in tomorrow at the Garden and Landscape Store?" Katy asked.

"Yes, please give him a call," Dave said in a raspy voice. "Tell him I will keep in touch with him through the week."

"Should I let Sheriff Jesse know you are sick?" Katy asked. "The investigation team is coming tomorrow at ten o'clock to walk through the underground tunnel of our home."

"You probably should," Dave answered. "He can decide if they should still come."

Katy walked over to the phone and dialed the number.

"Hello, this is Sheriff Jesse. How may I help you?" Sheriff Jesse asked.

"Hi, Sheriff Jesse, this is Katy Middleton."

"Hi, Katy, how are you and Dave getting along after that wonderful sledding party yesterday at Farmer Brown's?" Sheriff Jesse asked.

"That is the reason why I am calling, Sheriff Jesse," Katy answered. "Dave has come down with a sore throat, and he is sneezing a lot. Dave wanted me to call and let you know so you and the investigation team can make the decision on coming tomorrow to walk through that underground tunnel."

"I really appreciate that, Katy," Sheriff Jesse said. "I am sure it will be all right that we still come. Thank you for letting us know, and we will see you at ten o'clock tomorrow morning."

"Thank you, Sheriff Jesse. I will be watching for your arrival tomorrow morning," Katy said.

Chapter 9

At ten o'clock Monday morning, the bell on the front porch rang.

"Hi, Sheriff Jesse, come in," Katy said.

"How is Dave feeling?" Sheriff Jesse asked.

"A little better," Katy answered. "His temperature is back to normal, and he isn't coughing or sneezing as much."

"This is the investigation team," Sheriff Jesse said. "Ralph is the leader of the investigation team from Springfield, Oklahoma. They will be walking with Deputy James and me through the tunnel to see where it leads. Please leave everything open while we are down there. We may need to get out quickly. I have no idea what we might find at the end of that tunnel."

"Everything is open right now," Katy said. "You remember my parents, John and Mary Williamson."

"Yes, we came to their rescue when those intruders broke into your home during your honeymoon on the houseboat," Sheriff Jesse said.

"Good to see you again, Sheriff Jesse and Deputy James," Father and Mother Williamson said, shaking their hands.

"Hi, Dave, are you feeling any better?" Sheriff Jesse asked as he peeked around the corner into the sitting room.

"Better than yesterday. Thanks to my wonderful wife and her homemade chicken and vegetable noodle soup and fabulous vanilla malts," Dave said.

"I will let you know what we find in that underground tunnel," Sheriff Jesse said.

"I am anxious to hear all about it," Dave answered. "Sorry I can't help."

"You need to stay where it is warm," Sheriff Jesse said. "It is really cold in that tunnel. We don't want you catching bronchitis or pneumonia."

"Follow me, Sheriff Jesse," Katy said. Sheriff Jesse, Deputy James, Ralph, and the investigation team walked through the bookcase opening and went down the steep stairway to the padlocked door. Sheriff Jesse unlocked the padlock and opened the door. To their surprise, the door leading to the tunnel was wide open.

"Looks like somebody has been here," Deputy James said.

"They may still be here," Sheriff Jesse remarked with a concerned look on his face.

The investigation team had large spotlights that gave them plenty of light to see where they were going as they began walking through the tunnel.

"It is very clean in this tunnel," Deputy James said.

"There is no water or any type of condensation on the walls, ceiling, or floor," Sheriff Jesse remarked.

"This underground tunnel is encased in thick concrete," Ralph, the investigation team leader, said. "It is tough enough to withstand a bomb blast, a tornado, or even a missile strike."

After an hour of walking through the tunnel, they came to a large room where there was a small woodstove to cook on, a wooden table with four chairs, a large sofa, a pool table, and a large ice chest.

"Looks like someone has been living here," Ralph said.

"Perhaps it is a hideout where kids might hang out when they don't want to be found," Deputy James said.

"What's behind those large black curtains hanging on that wall?" Sheriff Jesse asked.

Ralph opened the black curtains, and they were shocked at what they saw.

"Two glass windows," Deputy James said.

"On the other side of the glass windows is a pressure-treated pine wall," Sheriff Jesse said.

"Sheriff, these aren't windows, they are sliding glass doors!" Deputy James said excitedly "What would you call this place?" he asked as he slid one of the glass doors open.

"It looks similar to concrete buildings called pavilions," Sheriff Jesse answered. "They are structures built underground with one side that has an opening to get in and out of."

Sheriff Jesse, Deputy James, and Ralph, the investigation team leader, stepped out on a narrow concrete ledge between the pressure-treated pine wall and glass doors.

"There are two heavy black chains on each side of this pressure-treated pine wall hooked to bars on top of the pavilion," Deputy James said. "We are going to need some assistance getting the two chains unhooked."

"I need three men to help us unhook two heavy chains," Ralph said. Tom, Don, and Rick from the investigation team stepped out on the ledge to help unhook the heavy chains from the heavy bar on top of the pavilion.

"I found a heavy crank on each side of the pavilion," Deputy James said.

Using all their strength, Sheriff Jesse turned the crank on the right side of the pavilion, and Deputy James turned the crank on the left side of the pavilion. The pressure-treated pine wall slowly moved downward and fell on top of the water with a loud splash. The heavy black chains were still attached to the crank apparatus on each side of the pavilion, keeping the pressure-treated pine wall from floating away.

"This is part of Cedar River that runs through Dark Woods," Sheriff Jesse said as he stepped onto the pressure-treated pine wall.

"Do you see a boat anywhere?" Deputy James asked.

"There probably would be a boat if someone was here," Ralph answered.

"The person or people have to get here somehow, Sheriff," Deputy James said.

"What do you want to do?" Ralph asked.

"We better place surveillance cameras outside and in this room," Sheriff Jesse suggested.

"Okay, I have all the equipment we need in the van," Ralph said. "I will send six men to go get it. That way, we can stay here. You never know when our mystery guest or guests may show up."

The men of the investigation team started walking through the tunnel to get the equipment from the van.

"Look! A rowboat!" Deputy James exclaimed. The three men looked around the area where the rowboat was hidden in a thicket of brush and bushes.

"I wonder what is on the other side of the river?" Sheriff Jesse asked. "Ralph, Deputy James and I are going to take that rowboat and take a look at what is on the other side of the river."

"Okay, I will stay here," Ralph replied. "It will be some time before the men get back with those surveillance cameras."

Deputy James and Sheriff Jesse got in the rowboat and started rowing their way across Cedar River.

"I sure hope this old rowboat doesn't have holes in it," Deputy James said with a concerned look on his face.

"If there were holes, the boat would have had water in it while it was sitting among the bushes and thicket," Sheriff Jesse said. "Why do you always wait until we are in the middle of a river and bring up the fact that the boat we are sitting in might have holes in it?" Sheriff Jesse asked.

"It doesn't concern me until I am in the middle of a river, lake, or pond," Deputy James answered. "When I was a boy, I was with my dad fishing on a friend's pond. We hadn't been there long, and suddenly, water started gushing inside the rowboat. We stopped fishing and started rowing that boat as fast as we could back to the dock. What was really scary were the four snapping turtles following us. I still have nightmares about that day."

In approximately thirty minutes, Sheriff Jesse and Deputy James had come to the riverbank. They were both amazed at what they saw.

"I had no idea there was a stone cottage in Dark Woods," Sheriff Jesse said.

"Doesn't look like anyone is living in it. The windows are boarded shut," Deputy James remarked. "You want to get out and look around?" Deputy James asked.

"No, not today," Sheriff Jesse answered. "I want to be back when they start putting those surveillance cameras in place. I would

like to take a stroll on this side of Cedar River this week and try to find this place."

"We might not be able to find it with all the trees and bushes surrounding it," Deputy James said.

"That's true, but it is worth a try," Sheriff Jesse said. "We better get back."

"Did you find anything on the other side of Cedar River?" Ralph asked anxiously.

"Yes, a stone cottage surrounded by many trees," Sheriff Jesse answered. "The windows were boarded up. Looks like no one has lived there for a while."

"Maybe that is who is coming to the pavilion and is using it as a hideout when they think they have been seen at the stone cottage," Ralph said.

"That could very well be," Sheriff Jesse said.

"What I can't figure out is why was a rowboat hidden in the bushes just outside of the pavilion entrance," Deputy James said.

"That is a very good question," Sheriff Jesse said.

"I think the person or persons are still using that stone cottage and are hiding somewhere around the pavilion at this very moment," Ralph said. "That could be why the rowboat was here. They could be watching us right now and know we have discovered the pavilion."

"Or they might have a motorboat, and the rowboat could be an extra boat for them to use in case their motorboat wouldn't start," Sheriff Jesse said.

"What makes you think they have a motorboat?" Deputy James asked.

"Just a hunch," Sheriff Jesse said, shrugging his shoulders. "Not too many people use a rowboat unless it is the last resort. Furthermore, just because the windows on that stone cottage were boarded up doesn't mean there isn't anyone living there."

"You are right, Sheriff. They might have had to go on a food run at one of the stops along Cedar River," Deputy James said.

"We definitely will be keeping an eye on that stone cottage in the days ahead," Sheriff Jesse said.

The six men returned within three hours to the large room of the pavilion with the surveillance equipment.

"Great! Start placing those cameras," Ralph said. "We don't want to be here after dark. There isn't any electricity in here."

The investigation team worked quickly in placing the surveillance cameras around the room and outside among the trees.

"That should do it, Ralph," said one of the team members.

"Be sure to crank that pressure-treated pine wall up and attach the hooks to the bar on top of the pavilion," Sheriff Jesse said.

"Slide those glass doors shut and close the black curtains," Ralph said as the last man stepped inside. "We want everything to look the way it was before we came."

Ralph, with his investigation team, Sheriff Jesse, and Deputy James walked quickly through the tunnel. The door to the tunnel was closed tightly, and the door leading to the room was closed and padlocked. After walking up the steep stairs, Sheriff Jesse dropped the floor back into place and closed the door under the oak stairway.

"Now what?" Deputy James asked.

"We will be watching our monitors in our office to see if anyone arrives and goes inside," Ralph said. "When this happens, we will be contacting you and Sheriff Jesse so you can arrest our mysterious visitors."

"We will be waiting for your call," Sheriff Jesse said.

"What would you call that concrete building?" Katy asked.

"I would call it a pavilion," Ralph answered. "It reminds me of a garden summerhouse."

"It might have been an area for the past owners to enjoy the outdoors in private, or it might have been a shelter they went to when bad storms occurred. It is on your property, and you own it," Sheriff Jesse said. "Anyone else going inside is trespassing."

"It is a safe place to go if a tornado comes through," Deputy James said.

"The only thing keeping these mysterious visitors from coming into your home is the door that is padlocked at the bottom of the stairway," Ralph said.

"Be sure to keep that door padlocked," Sheriff Jesse said.

"Thank you for coming, and please keep us informed also," Katy said. "I am going to tell Dave everything."

Dave was amazed when Katy told him what the investigation team found at the end of the underground tunnel.

"There might not be anyone coming inside that pavilion," Dave said. "My grandparents probably built it so they would have a safe place to go when the storms went through Sweetwater."

"They have to know for sure, Dave. That is why cameras were put up," Katy said.

"You are right. We need to see if anyone is trespassing on our property," Dave said.

"Would you like something to eat?" Katy asked.

"I am hungry for a double cheeseburger, french fries, and a hot fudge sundae with nuts," Dave said.

"You are feeling better," Katy said. "I can make all that for you, Dave. I will go to the kitchen and get it ready." Then she asked, "Mother, Father, would you like the same?"

"Sounds good to me," Father Williamson said.

"I will help you prepare it," Mother Williamson said.

Chapter 10

It was the middle of February. Valentine's Day was coming up.

"Do you realize, Katy, Valentine's Day will soon be here and it will be our first Valentine's Day celebration together?" Dave said.

"You are right!" Katy exclaimed. "There is going to be a Valentine's Day party at the Sweetwater Public Library Wednesday. I need to make a box for Chester's valentines to be placed in. I made a copy of his right paw print. That is what I used as Chester's signature on the valentines he is giving the children at the party."

"They will certainly like that," Dave said. "You come up with very good ideas to make the children of Sweetwater, Oklahoma, happy."

"I plan to pick up the decorated valentine cookies and heart-shaped cake at Miss Emily's bakery on Library Day," Katy said.

"I am looking forward to seeing the valentines the children give to Chester," Dave said.

"I am looking forward to it too," Katy said. "It will be an exciting and fun day."

"What would you like to do to celebrate our first Valentine's Day together?" Dave asked.

"Surprise me!" exclaimed Katy.

"Keep this weekend open," Dave said.

"I will," Katy said.

Katy was giving Chester's valentine box her final touch as Chester walked into the kitchen.

"Today is Library Day, Chester," Katy said as she pasted a picture of Chester on top of the valentine box. Katy wrapped the box in red glitter tissue paper. "One more thing to do," Katy said as she picked up scissors. She carefully cut a wide opening at the top of the box. "Voilà! Your valentine box is ready!" exclaimed Katy.

"Chester, ride!" Katy shouted. Chester immediately ran to his white cupboard in the kitchen and got his collar. "We are off to the library, Chester," Katy said as she locked the door. "First, we need to stop at Ms. Emily's bakery for the cookies and the cake and then it will be party time!"

Party time! I love parties. I remember the Halloween and Christmas parties at the library. I am very excited! More attention and goodies for me. I have a wonderful life! thought Chester.

"Hi, Katy and Chester," Miss Lilly said with a pleasant welcome smile. "Let me help you with the cake and cookies."

"Thank you," Katy said.

"The children will be arriving soon," Miss Lilly said. "I have a table set up for the valentine boxes. When the children arrive, they may start placing their valentines in the boxes."

"I love what you did," Katy said, looking around the room. "The red vinyl tablecloth with white and pink glitter hearts dangling at the bottom looks fabulous."

"Thank you," Miss Lilly said.

"Look, Chester, the children are arriving," Katy said in an anxious voice. "Let's go greet them and show them where to place their valentine box."

"All right, children, if any of you have not placed your valentines in the boxes on the table, now would be a good time to do so," Miss Lilly said. "After you do that, please come and sit down. Katy will read the story *The Runaway Valentine*."

"The children sure were excited today," Katy said as the last child walked down the library steps to their car.

"The heart-shaped valentine with accordion arms and legs as their craft turned out so cute. I knew it would be a great success! Don't forget Chester and your valentine boxes," Miss Lilly said as she handed the valentine boxes to Katy. "Here are some cookies and cake for Dave and you to enjoy."

"Thank you, Miss Lilly," Katy said. "See you next Wednesday."

"Yes, next Wednesday at one o'clock," Miss Lilly said as she waved goodbye.

That was some party. These parties at the library seem to get better and better. I can't wait for the next one. I wonder what celebration is coming up next. Maybe Samson will know, thought Chester as he watched out the car window heading home.

"Well, Chester, we have a busy night ahead of us," Katy said as she drove the SUV into the driveway in front of the house. "Dave is going to want to see our valentines and hear everything about the party."

We can't forget Samson. Samson will want to know too. I need to give Samson a valentine. Oh no, I don't have any idea how to make a valentine. Oh, look, here is one last valentine with my paw print on it. I will give this valentine to Samson, thought Chester.

"We are home, Katy," Dave said.

"Fantastic! I can't wait to tell you about the valentines party," Katy said.

Dave placed Samson on the floor, and Chester walked up to him with his valentine in his mouth.

"Happy Valentine's Day, friend," Chester said.

"Thank you! Pretty card," said Samson.

"What a friendship those two have," Dave said.

"I am so glad they get along like they do," Katy said.

Chapter 11

It was Friday, the day before Valentine's Day. Dave had left for work with Samson on his shoulder. Katy was looking out the window in the sitting room.

I wonder if Dave remembers Valentine's Day tomorrow, thought Katy. Just then the bell rang from the front porch. Katy opened the door, and a tall man holding a long white rectangle box and a small white square box was standing on the porch. "Katy Middleton?" he asked.

"Yes, I am Katy Middleton," Katy answered.

"I have a delivery for you. Please sign that you accept and have received it," the delivery man said, handing a pen and clipboard to Katy. Katy hurriedly signed her name and took the two boxes and a copy of the signed receipt.

"What could this be?" she asked herself as she quickly walked to the kitchen. Katy opened the white square box. Inside was a red heart-shaped box with a red flowery bow on top. She lifted the top off and saw the assortment of chocolates. Katy then untied the red ribbon around the long white rectangle box. Carefully lifting the top from the box, she saw twelve red roses inside. A card, which was inside, said thus:

> To my darling wife, Katy,
> who I love with all my heart!
> I will be home at five o'clock this afternoon.
> Be hungry and have your dancing shoes on.
> Scott and Peggy will watch Chester and Samson.
> They plan to celebrate their Valentine's Day on
> Saturday.
> See you soon!
> Love, Dave

Katy twirled around with excitement. She placed the red roses in a large vase of water and sat them in the sitting room for all to enjoy.

I better make something special for Scott and Peggy to munch on while they are here, thought Katy. She prepared her "cherries in the snow" dessert and made a dozen homemade buns and a platter of sliced ham and cheese. She had just taken a large jelly roll pan of caramel corn out of the oven. The grandfather clock in the sitting room suddenly struck three times. "It is already three o'clock in the afternoon!" Katy exclaimed to herself. "I need to start getting ready. Dave will be home in two hours."

"I'm home, honey!" Dave shouted as he put Samson down on the floor. Samson walked through the hallway with his feet, going clickety-clack, clickety-clack and saying, "Buddy! Buddy! Where are you? I'm home, honey!"

I am not your honey! I am your pal, your buddy, your friend, Samson. Oh well, just go with the flow. I don't want to hurt Samson's feelings, thought Chester.

Katy was slipping her red heels on her feet when Dave walked into the bedroom.

"Hey, gorgeous!" Dave exclaimed. "Are you ready for a wild night?" Dave asked. "Scott and Peggy are on their way," Dave said as he hurried to the bathroom to take a shower.

"A wild night?" Katy asked with a shocked look on her face.

Katy heard the bell ring on the front porch and ran to let Scott and Peggy in. "Help yourselves to the food I prepared for you," Katy said. Dave came walking into the sitting room and handed Katy a heart-shaped red velvet box. "What is this?" Katy asked.

"Open it and find out," Dave said.

Katy gasped when she opened the box and saw the red ruby necklace, earrings, bracelet, and ring.

The angel wing love heart red ruby necklace, earrings, and ring were stunning and attractive, glittering and sparkling. Diamonds surrounded each ruby, and a diamond was encased in the upper center of each ruby. Gold resembling angel wings surrounded the diamonds on each ruby of the necklace, earrings, and ring. The attractive bracelet displayed glistening oval-cut red rubies set in between a polished and white studded swirl design with a diamond in between each ruby. The dazzling set represented the symbol of *forever love* that reveals the giver's endless style. Being eye-catching and luxurious, it was an amazing gift for Katy by that special someone in her life, Dave, her husband.

"They are beautiful, Dave," Katy said, giving him a kiss.

"Oh, Katy, they will look fantastic with your red dress and heels," Peggy said. "Let me help you with your necklace."

"Thank you, Peggy," Katy said.

"You really outdid yourself, buddy," Scott said.

"We are off!" Dave said, taking hold of Katy's arm.

"Make yourself at home," Katy said.

"Have a good time," said Scott and Peggy together.

"We have reservations at Johnny and Frankie's in Springwater, Oklahoma," Dave said. When Katy walked into the restaurant, she was impressed by how romantic everything was. Miniature starlights were twinkling throughout the room. The waiter escorted them to their table and took their order. "I will have a rib eye steak, medium rare, baked potato with butter, and Italian dressing on my salad," Dave said.

"And you, madam?" the waiter asked.

"I would like the same," answered Katy.

"What would you like to drink?" the waiter asked.

"Please bring a glass of water with a lemon wedge for both of us," Dave said.

"Dave, isn't this rather expensive?" Katy said with a concerned look on her face.

"Nothing is too expensive for you," Dave answered.

"Everything is absolutely beautiful here," Katy remarked. "The music is very relaxing. I had no idea this place was here."

"It just opened up," Dave said. "I had to make reservations since this was our first Valentine's Day together. I wanted our first Valentine's Day to be really special."

"I will remember this forever, Dave," Katy said.

"We have one more stop after this," Dave said. "I have reservations at the ballroom, a few blocks from here."

"How exciting," Katy said.

"The band starts playing at nine o'clock," Dave said.

"I have heard a lot about the ballroom but have never been there," Katy said.

"We better get going," Dave said as he held Katy's coat while she slipped it on.

The ballroom was extravagant. A clerk checked in their coats. A greeter escorted Dave and Katy to a booth. A dish of heart candies and a red rose in a vase of water was placed in the center of the table. Red hearts with lights danced through the air, on the ceiling, and on the dance floor. Dave and Katy danced to every slow song the band played. The last song was "I Love You Truly."

"Oh, Dave, this is the song I played on my violin at our wedding," Katy said.

"It sure is," Dave said, holding her tight and kissing her on the lips.

As Dave opened the car door, Katy said, "I will always remember our first Valentine's Day together." Later, traveling outside of Springville, Oklahoma, Katy said, "Dave, could you stop at a convenience store and pick up a quart of milk. I don't have enough milk to make pancakes tomorrow. I thought Scott and Peggy would like a good breakfast before leaving tomorrow morning."

"Sure," Dave said as he pulled into Hank's Quick Shop. Katy waited in the car. Dave was walking to the cash register to pay for the milk. Suddenly, two large men with ski masks walked in, waving a .22 caliber pistol at the cashier.

"Give me all your money in the register," said the man wearing the blue ski mask.

"Do you have a vault?" asked the man in the black ski mask.

"No, everything in the cash register is all we have," the cashier answered. "Please, oh please, don't shoot me!" the cashier exclaimed. "Here, take all of it and be on your way!"

The two men then looked at Dave.

"What are you staring at?" the man in the black ski mask asked.

Dave stood silently with his quart of milk.

"What's the matter? Cat got your tongue?" said the man wearing the blue ski mask, laughing loudly.

The two men shot their guns in the air and turned around, rushing through the door. Katy sat very still in the car, hoping the two men would not see her. Then she saw Dave drop to the floor. The two men got into their truck and drove away. Katy jumped out of the car and ran inside. A bullet had ricocheted from a shelf and landed in Dave's chest. The cashier instantly called 911.

"Oh, Dave, darling, please don't die," Katy said with tears running down her face. Katy saw blood gushing from Dave's chest. The cashier handed Katy a towel from a shelf under the counter. Katy pressed the towel against Dave's chest where the bullet had gone in. The ambulance arrived within fifteen minutes. Katy rode in the ambulance and continued to talk to Dave so he would stay awake. The ambulance drove to the emergency entrance at the Methodist Hospital in Springville, Oklahoma. Katy called Scott and Peggy at the house immediately.

"Dave has been shot," Katy said, whimpering as she spoke. "We are at the Methodist Hospital in Springville. He is in surgery now, having the bullet removed from his chest."

"Oh, Katy, how can I help?" Peggy asked.

"I need Scott to take Samson to the store tomorrow morning," Katy said.

"I will grab Chester and come to the hospital to be with you," Peggy said. "I will call the vet emergency number to let them know I will be dropping Chester off at the vet clinic."

"Thanks, Peggy!" Katy said. "Drive safe! I am going to call my parents now."

Chapter 12

Katy dropped the correct coins in the pay phone hanging on the wall in the emergency waiting room of the Methodist Hospital. She dialed her parents' phone number.

"The Williamsons!" came a sleepy response at the other end.

"Hello, Mother, it's Katy!"

"Katy, do you realize it is three o'clock in the morning?" Mother Williamson said.

"Yes, I am sorry to be calling at this hour, but I have some bad news," Katy said, trying her best to hold back the tears. "Dave is at the Methodist Hospital in Springville, undergoing surgery. A bullet ricocheted from a shelf in a convenience store and landed in Dave's chest. We were on our way home from a Valentine's Day celebration."

"Oh my, which side of his chest?" Mother Williamson asked.

"The right side," Katy answered as she started to cry. "I am worried he may become paralyzed."

"We will come to the hospital and be with you," Mother Williamson replied. "We are already praying for the both of you."

"Mother, please take care driving to Springville," Katy said softly. "I don't need Father and you in the hospital too."

"Don't you worry about us, my sweet daughter. We will be fine," Mother Williamson said in a comforting voice.

"I am very worried, Mother," Katy said in a very weak voice.

"We will be there soon," Mother Williamson said. "What about Chester and Samson?" she asked.

"Peggy is taking Chester to the veterinarian's clinic in Springville so he can be with the other cats," Katy said. "I don't think Chester will be allowed in the hospital. Scott is taking Samson to the Garden and Landscape Store this morning."

"I will pack some clothes for your father and myself, and we will be on our way," Mother Williamson said.

*****

"Hey, Peggy!" shouted Scott. "Samson and I are leaving. Keep me posted by calling me."

"I will do that," Peggy said. "Chester, ride!" Peggy shouted as she stood at the front door. Chester had just finished his breakfast and ran to his white cupboard for his collar. "Come on, Chester, we are driving to Springville," Peggy said. "I am going to take you to the veterinarian clinic in Springville so you can play with the kitties. Someone will be picking you up soon."

Chester walked into the room, where five cats were walking around and playing tag with each other.

"What are you in for?" asked a large black cat.

"Something happened to Dave, my best friend. He is in the hospital. My owner, Katy, is with him," said Chester.

"Oh, that's too bad," the large black cat said. "My name is Butch."

"Hi, my name is Peachy," said a medium-sized calico cat.

"Nice to meet you," Chester said.

"I am not feeling well either," said the medium-sized calico cat, Peachy. "I need to get rid of one of those hair balls too."

"Really, you are going to go there!" exclaimed the large black cat, Butch. "Humans don't cough up hair balls, silly!"

"Oh!" said the medium-sized calico cat, Peachy.

"Why are you wearing that white cap and jacket?" Chester asked.

"I am a purrmedic," Peachy answered. "Do you need assistance in calming down, Chester?" Peachy asked.

"Calm down! This isn't my first time here. I have been here many times, and there has been no reason for having assistance in calming down, Purrmedic Peachy. Thank you for offering, but no thank you," Chester said, looking annoyed.

"Just doing my job, Chester," Purrmedic Peachy said as she quietly walked away.

In walked a cat that looked just like Chester but was smaller in size.

"Hi! My name is Chucky. You can call me Chuck."

"Hi, my name is Chester. You can call me Chester," said Chester.

"I hear you got a sick one in your family," Chucky said. "Pity, what a shame. It doesn't look good for you, Chester. You might be staying here for a while. That is probably why they dropped you off here."

"No way!" said Chester, giving a twirl with his body and an angry meow. *"Katy and Dave would never leave me here. Samson would miss me. I am his buddy. Grammy and Grampy wouldn't hear of it either,"* said Chester.

"Who is Samson?" asked the black cat, Butch.

"My buddy and true friend. He is a cockatoo," Chester answered, looking very disgusted.

"Are there any kids?" asked the medium-sized calico cat, Peachy.

"Kids?" asked Chester.

"Yes, little people who grow up to be big people," stated the medium-sized calico cat, Peachy.

"No, nothing like that lives at our house. Just Samson, a cockatoo. He is a real pal. We are best friends," answered Chester as he walked away and curled up in the corner of the room to be alone.

As Peggy and Katy were talking in the waiting room, Mother and Father Williamson came rushing in.

"How is he doing?" Mother Williamson asked.

"I haven't heard. He is still in surgery," Katy said.

"John, go get Katy a glass of cold water," Mother Williamson said.

"Sure will. Can I get you anything else?" Father Williamson asked.

"No, not right now, thank you, Father," Katy said.

As Katy took a sip of her water, her mother took hold of her hand. "We need to join hands and form a circle and pray silently that Dave will be all right," Mother Williamson said humbly. After praying, Katy began telling Mother, Father, and Peggy what had happened at the convenience store. The doctor walked into the waiting room.

"Hello, my name is Dr. Rufus. Dave is in intensive care. We were able to remove the bullet from his chest, but he is in a coma. You may take turns going in to see him. Only one person at a time, and don't stay any longer than ten minutes. Talk to him. Talk about memories and all the good events that have happened in Dave's life. It is believed that people in a coma can still hear what is being said."

"Katy, you go in first, then your father and I will take our turn," Mother Williamson said. Katy walked into Dave's room. She fought back the tears as she walked up beside Dave. She gave him a gentle kiss on his cheek. Dave made no sound or movement.

"Hi, Dave, it's Katy. You need to wake up. Samson, Chester, and I need you. I should never have asked you to stop at that convenience store for a quart of milk. I am so sorry. It is all my fault." Katy then sat down in a chair and broke down in tears. Nurse Jane walked into the room and put her arms around Katy.

"Katy, you need to go home and get some rest," Nurse Jane said. "We will let you know if there is any change." Nurse Jane kindly escorted Katy out of the room.

Father Williamson took his turn next. He held Dave's hand and said, "Well, buddy, I know you are strong, and I know you can get through this. We have some planning to do for that garden at your house this spring. Don't forget about that underground tunnel at your house. I know you want to hear about that. I need to go now so Mother can come in and see you."

Mother Williamson took her turn last and walked into the room. "Hi, Dave. We are all praying for your recovery. Katy really needs you. Dave. She loves you very much. Father and I love you too. Please wake up soon. We will be back tomorrow."

"Let's let him rest now," Nurse Jane said. "You should all go home and get some rest. Keep your strength up and take care of yourselves. Come back tomorrow. You may call the hospital any time to find out if there is any change, and the hospital will call you immediately if there is a change."

"I don't want to leave him," Katy said. "He might wake up. I want to be here when he wakes up."

"Katy, you are exhausted," Mother Williamson said, placing her arm around Katy's waist. "You have not slept since getting up at six o'clock in the morning yesterday. You need to go home and sleep, or you will be in the hospital also."

"All right, I want to tell Dave good night," Katy said.

Katy walked into Dave's room and kissed him on the lips. "Good night, darling. I will be back soon," Katy said.

"I will see you at your home," Peggy said. "I just called Scott and told him to take Samson back to your house after he closes the store at noon."

"Thank you, Peggy, for being here and all the help you have given," Katy said. "It would have been a long night waiting by myself."

"That's what friends are for," Peggy answered. "I will pick Chester up at the veterinarian's clinic so you don't have to stop."

"Katy, we need to stop at the convenience store and pick up your car," Mother Williamson said. "Your father can drive your car, and you can ride with me in our car."

"Thank you, Mother," Katy said.

Later, driving in front of the house, Scott was standing on the porch.

"Let me help you with that," Scott offered as he picked up Mother and Father Williamson's luggage.

"Thank you, Scott," Mother and Father Williamson said together.

I am so glad to be home. I knew Katy wouldn't leave me at the vets. Samson, where are you, buddy, ole pal, true friend? Chester thought, running up the front porch steps and through the front door.

"Samson cracker! Samson cracker!" screeched Samson as he quickly walked through the hall, making the clickety-clack, clickety-clack sound with his feet to the kitchen.

"Really, Samson, that is all you have to say to me after being away from me for hours. Don't you realize a member of our family isn't here?" said Chester.

Scott carried Mother and Father Williamson's luggage up the spiral stairway to the guest room.

Mother Williamson and Peggy heated the homemade tomato bisque soup and prepared grilled cheese sandwiches and chocolate/vanilla swirl pudding. Father Williamson and Scott brought in more firewood and restarted the fireplaces. Chester was finishing a bowl of chicken and gravy, and Samson was finishing a bowl of bird seed. Katy walked into the kitchen as Mother Williamson was setting the table.

"Something sure smells yummy," Katy said.

"Sit at the table, all of you," Mother Williamson said as she filled the last glass with water and placed a lemon wedge on the rim of the glass. "Chester and Samson have eaten and are in the sitting room, enjoying the warm fire and cartoons on television."

"John, please give grace."

"Let's bow our heads," Father Williamson said. "Dear heavenly Father, bless this food that family and friends are about to eat. Watch over us and give us the strength to cope with what has happened to Dave. Watch over Dave. Heal him with your glorious healing hands, and may he wake up from his coma soon. In Jesus's name, amen."

"This is delicious, Mrs. Williamson," Peggy said.

"Yes, really warms a guy up on a cold day like today," Scott said.

"Thank you. Glad you like it," Mother Williamson said. "Katy is the one who should get the compliment. She made this tomato bisque soup. I just heated it up."

Katy sat quietly at the table, not hearing anything being said.

"Katy, you need to eat something," Mother Williamson said in a concerned voice.

"I just don't seem to be hungry," Katy said as she stirred through the tomato bisque soup with her spoon. "I feel I should be at the hospital in case Dave wakes up," Katy said as tears started falling from her eyes.

"Katy, you need to keep your strength up, so eat a little and then off to bed with you," Father Williamson said kindly. "You have been up for over twenty-four hours. Get rested up, and I will take you to the hospital tomorrow."

"Your father and I will take turns driving you to the hospital," Mother Williamson said.

"If you like, Katy, I will come for Samson every morning during the week so he can stay on his usual schedule going to the Garden and Landscape Store," Scott offered.

"That would be great," Katy said. "Thank you for everything all you have done. I truly appreciate it, and I know Dave appreciates it too. I am going to relax in the whirlpool tub and then go to bed," Katy said as she got up from the table and walked to her lavish bathroom.

Sitting on the outside of the whirlpool tub, Katy turned the hot-and-cold knobs to the on position. She placed her hands under the warm flowing water as the whirlpool tub began to fill. She began to pray to her Lord Jesus Christ, "Dear heavenly Father, you are the Creator, and you are the re-Creator as well. Please recreate in Dave the health, the strength, and the energy you gave him when you created him. Give him the healing grace of our Lord Jesus Christ, and please let him awake from his coma and make him well again. In Jesus's name, amen."

Scott and Peggy left after lunch. Father and Mother Williamson cleaned the dishes.

"It has been a long day," Father Williamson said.

"Yes, it has. I am tired also," Mother Williamson said.

"I will be upstairs after I put Samson in his cage," Father Williamson said. "Come on, Samson and Chester."

"Samson tired! Samson tired!" said Samson as he walked down the hall to the music room and settled down in his cage. Chester followed him and curled up beside the harp. "Both of you sleep well," Father Williamson said as he latched the door on Samson's cage.

"*Samson! Pssst! Samson! I want to sleep with Katy since Dave is gone. Do you want to come with me?*" Chester asked.

"Samson out! Samson out!" shouted Samson.

"*Hold on, buddy. I have to get this door open. There, out you go. Now I need to latch the door shut. Got it! Follow me!*" Chester said. Samson and Chester walked quietly over the soft carpet in Katy's bedroom. "*Samson, you stand on the dresser or at the foot of the bed,*"

Chester said. Samson let his wings spread out and flew to the foot of the bed. Chester carefully jumped on the bed and curled up beside Katy. Everyone slept through the night.

Chapter 13

Mother Williamson was busy preparing maple and brown sugar oatmeal. Two English muffins had just popped up from the toaster.

"Oh, I hear someone coming down the hall," Mother Williamson said as she finished spreading butter on the two English muffins.

Clickety-clack, clickety-clack went Samson's feet as he walked into the kitchen. "Samson cracker! Samson cracker!"

"Samson, you can't trick Grammy," Mother Williamson said. "I know you eat your breakfast before you can have a cracker."

"Good morning, Chester," Father Williamson said, seeing Chester walk slowly into the kitchen. "You still look tired. Your eyes aren't all the way open."

"Here are your egg and cheese bits with white sauce and a fresh bowl of cool water," Mother Williamson said as she placed the bowls in front of the white cupboard. "Perhaps that will wake you up," Mother Williamson said.

"I got the fire going again in the sitting room," Father Williamson replied. "We probably won't be attending church services this morning. I am sure Katy will want to go to the hospital."

"Yes, I am sure she will," Mother Williamson said as she placed a bowl of oatmeal on the table.

Katy had just finished smoothing the kaleidoscope design quilt on the king-size four-poster bed. *I am so pleased with this quilt that Dave chose when we spent our honeymoon on the houseboat,* Katy thought, blinking back tears. "Good morning, Mother and Father," Katy said as she walked into the kitchen.

"Did you sleep well, dear?" Mother Williamson asked.

"Yes, I slept through the night," Katy said.

"I will fix some oatmeal and English muffins for you," Mother Williamson said.

"I'm not hungry, Mother," Katy said.

"You need to eat a little. We don't want you in the hospital too," Father Williamson said.

"What time would you like to go to the hospital?" Mother Williamson asked.

"As soon as I eat, shower, and get dressed," Katy answered.

"Your father will be taking you," Mother Williamson said. "I will stay with Chester and Samson. Be sure to call me if there is any change and if Dave wakes up from his coma."

"We will do that," Katy said.

Mother and Father Williamson cleaned up the breakfast dishes. Katy had just finished grooming Chester. "Okay, Father, I am ready to go," Katy said.

"Be sure to drink plenty of liquids and eat something while you are there," Mother Williamson said. "You don't want to get run-down or get sick. Your husband needs you to stay healthy. Keep thinking positive and pray."

"Thank you, Mother," Katy said as she put her coat on. "We will be taking my SUV. That way, you have your vehicle if you need anything. Remember, all you have to say is 'ride,' and Chester will get his collar and be off with you to the car. Don't forget his black leash. Placing the leash on Chester will keep him from wandering here and there. He can be very curious sometimes."

"I don't think we will be going anywhere," Mother Williamson replied. "I wouldn't want to leave Samson alone in the house, and I want to stay close to the phone. I will write a note to remind you to call Miss Lilly at the public library that you won't be able to come and read to the children this week," Mother Williamson said as she kissed Katy on the cheek.

"That is a good idea. Thank you, Mother," Katy said as she waved goodbye.

Katy and her father arrived at the Methodist Hospital in Springville, Oklahoma, at ten o'clock. Pastor Mike was coming out of Dave's room and saw Katy walking down the hall.

"Hi, Katy and Mr. Williamson," Pastor Mike said, shaking their hands. "I have been talking to Dave about the good times we have had at the church picnics, potlucks and ice cream socials. I reminded him of his favorite—your apple pie, Katy. I also brought up when we were filling in the Sugar Creek behind the church so we could make a cemetery. Louis Mulberry was leaning over and fell in the water of the creek. He didn't get hurt, but he sure was covered with mud and really drenched with water. I read a passage from the Bible and said a prayer with him."

"How kind and thoughtful of you," Katy said happily. "There still is no change?" she asked.

"No, the nurse told me they changed his bedding and gave him a bed bath this morning," Pastor Mike answered. "There has been no response from him. I have told members of our congregation, and they are all praying for Dave, you, and your family. Their thoughts and prayers are with all of you, Katy," Pastor Mike said.

"Thank you!" Katy said.

"If there is any change, please let me know," Pastor Mike said.

"I will," Katy answered.

Chapter 14

As the weeks went by, there was no change in Dave coming out of the coma. Katy would go to the hospital every day. She would talk about finding Chester under a bridge in a park, how she first met Dave, Dave and Scott planting the four purple lilac bushes on her property, attending church and the delicious potlucks at the Sugar Creek Country Church, their first picnic at Twin Cedar Bridges Park where Dave enjoyed eating Katy's fried chicken, potato salad, apple pie, and ice cold lemonade along with the ice cream Dave bought when the cart driven by a man on bicycle came strolling down the pathway for the first time, finding the third-story room in the yellow Victorian house, the intruders who broke into the house while they were going through the items that were stored on the third-story home, the large harp that had the glitter gold card hanging from one of its strings, which was from Dave's grandmother, the white shed Dave painted and placed yellow shutters around the windows and a tile floor with barn boards on the walls inside, the gazebo Dave spray painted, front porch Dave painted, Sheriff Jesse being kidnapped and rescued from the barn he had been placed in, the church ice cream social, Dave's marriage proposal to her at the Springfield, Oklahoma Fair on the Ferris wheel, their wedding day in October, the seven days on the houseboat for their honeymoon, the intruders breaking into their home a second time while they were on their honeymoon, the Halloween mystery that was solved in Dark Woods, Thanksgiving gathering at Mother and Father's Williamsons' home in Oklahoma City, Oklahoma, their first Christmas together, going caroling, the New Year's Eve party, the cockatoo, Samson, becoming a member of their family, the sledding party at Farmer Brown's farm, their first Valentines celebration, the tunnel leading to a pavilion, eating at

Sammy's Sugar Shack in Sweetwater, Oklahoma, how Samson, the cockatoo, is always out of his cage and an open cracker box is often found on the kitchen counter every morning with a cracker missing. As Katy talked to Dave, she wrote all the memories down. She thought it would be nice to refer back to them in the future, especially if she and Dave wanted to start a family.

"Good morning, Katy," Dr. Rufus said.

"Good morning, Doctor Rufus," Katy answered. "There doesn't seem to be any change in Dave's condition," Katy said as she broke down in tears.

"Katy, come with me to my office," Dr. Rufus said. "I would like to speak with you in private."

"May my father come too?" Katy asked as Father Williamson walked in with two cups of coffee. "Sure, follow me," Dr. Rufus said.

"Have a seat," Dr. Rufus said. Katy and Father Williamson each sat down on large black leather wingback chairs that stood in front of Dr. Rufus's desk. "You seem very depressed," Dr. Rufus said. "What is going on?" Dr. Rufus asked.

"I try to stay positive and keep from crying, but I just can't seem to do that," Katy said in a whimpering voice.

"Who has come to see Dave while he has been in a coma?" Dr. Rufus asked.

"My parents, members of the Sugar Creek Lutheran Church, including Pastor Mike, Scott, Dave's assistant at the Garden and Landscape Store, Peggy, Scott's girlfriend, every business owner and worker of Sweetwater," Katy said. "He gets a lot of company, Dr. Rufus. They all talk to him about memories, laugh about times that happened in the past, even events before Dave and I met."

"That sounds encouraging," Dr. Rufus said, smiling. "Have Dave's relatives been notified?" Dr. Rufus asked.

"Dave doesn't have any relatives," Katy answered. "He survived a car accident as a child and grew up in homes under foster care in Oklahoma."

"Do you have any pets?" Dr. Rufus asked.

"Yes, a Maine coon cat whose name is Chester and a cockatoo named Samson," Katy said.

"Does Dave get along with this cat and bird?" Dr. Rufus asked.

"Yes, Dave met Chester the same day I met him at his Garden and Landscape Store in Sweetwater," Katy said. "And Samson has been with us since the day after Christmas," Katy said.

"I see," Dr. Rufus said, raising his eyebrows and twitching his mouth. "Has Chester and Samson been to the hospital with you to see Dave?" Dr. Rufus asked.

"No, Chester and Samson have not been to the hospital," Katy said.

"I see," Dr. Rufus said, raising his eyebrows and twitching his mouth again. "This is only a suggestion, Katy," Dr. Rufus said with a smile on his face. "Bring Chester and Samson to the hospital with you during your next visit."

"Why?" Katy asked.

"It has been known that pets can do marvelous things when loved ones are hurting or are sick," Dr. Rufus answered. "I am not saying you and all the other visitors have not been doing good when coming to see Dave. All of you have been outstanding in doing a fantastic job talking to him. Pets have their own way of making adults and children, who are ill or depressed, feel better. Tomorrow is Sunday. Come in the morning. Not many visitors are present during that time. If you have any trouble with the nurses, have them page me."

"I will give it a try," Katy said. "I know Chester and Samson will want to see Dave, and I am very excited to see what happens!" Katy exclaimed.

"Good. See you tomorrow morning," Dr. Rufus said. "Take care of yourselves."

"Thank you, Dr. Rufus," Katy said. "We appreciate all you are doing for Dave."

"Yes, thank you," Father Williamson said, shaking his hand.

"Wouldn't it be wonderful if Chester and Samson could wake Dave up?" Katy said.

"Don't get your hopes up, honey," Father Williamson said as he was driving toward the town of Sweetwater, Oklahoma. "I have heard stories about dogs coming to the hospital to visit people who are ill. They seem to give the people a different outlook on life and are able to improve tremendously and get well in no time. I have never heard of other pets waking a person in a coma."

"Well, we will soon find out Sunday morning," Katy said excitedly. "Let's stop and have something to eat at Sammy's Sugar Shack," Katy suggested. "My treat!" Katy exclaimed.

"Okay," Father Williamson said.

"Let's not tell anyone that we plan to take Chester and Samson to the hospital tomorrow morning," Katy said. "I don't want a lot of curious people showing up."

"That is a good idea," Father Williamson replied. "It should be you, your mother, and I. Too many might make Chester and Samson nervous."

"Yes, and Samson needs to stay calm," Katy said.

"I sure hope there isn't anyone at the hospital named Goliath," Father Williamson said, chuckling.

"Oh my, that is all we need to have to happen," Katy replied, giggling.

Chapter 15

Chester and Samson had finished eating their breakfast and were on their way to the sitting room to watch the sun come up on a beautiful Sunday morning.

"Katy, you need to get ready," Mother Williamson said. "We want to be at the hospital before ten o'clock this morning."

"You are going with us, aren't you, Mother?" Katy asked.

"I wouldn't miss this for anything!" Mother Williamson exclaimed as she hurried to clear the breakfast dishes from the table.

"Chester, ride," Katy said as she waited by the front door.

"Come on, Samson, fly to my shoulder," Father Williamson said. "We are going to visit Dave."

"Chester and Samson, we are going to the hospital to see Dave," Katy said as they traveled in the SUV toward Methodist Hospital in Springville, Oklahoma. "Dave is asleep, and I hope you can wake him." Chester listened carefully as Katy ran her fingers through his thick orange hair.

"Samson, cracker! Samson, cracker!" squawked Samson.

"Samson, you know we don't eat in the car," Katy said sternly. "You may have a cracker at the hospital." Samson ruffled his feathers outward and then settled down to enjoy the view as he looked through the back window.

As Father Williamson drove in front of the hospital entrance doors, a car attendant opened the doors of the SUV. As everyone exited the SUV, the car attendant gave Father Williamson a small card with the number 3-25 on it. This number told the car attendant where to find the SUV when Father Williamson and his passengers would be ready to leave the hospital. The car attendant drove the SUV to a three-story parking ramp.

"Okay, Chester and Samson, you must be very good in the hospital," Katy said softly. "We are going to see Dave."

"Dave! Dave! Samson work! Samson work," squawked Samson.

"Samson, please be quiet," Katy said, shaking her index finger at Samson. "We don't want to disturb any of the other patients in the hospital."

Katy walked to the information desk.

"Hi, I am Katy Middleton. Doctor Rufus wanted my mother, father, Chester, Samson, and me to visit my husband, David Middleton, this morning."

"Oh, yes, I read that when I arrived at work today," the receptionist answered. "Do you know the way to your husband's room?" the receptionist asked.

"Yes, thank you," Katy answered. "Would you have a cart I could use?" Katy asked. "The cage that Samson is in is quite heavy for my father to carry."

"Yes, I do," the receptionist answered. "Please wait here. I will be back momentarily." Within fifteen minutes, the receptionist was walking toward Father Williamson, pushing a tall stainless steel cart. "This should be perfect for the cage that your cockatoo is in," the receptionist said with a pleased smile while Mother and Father Williamson placed the cage on the top of the cart.

"Thank you for all your assistance," Katy said graciously.

"My name is Anne," the receptionist said. "If I can help you with anything else, please let me know. Have a wonderful visit with Dave."

"Thank you," Mother and Father Williamson said together.

"Thank you, Anne! Thank you, Anne! Want to go out tonight? Want to go out tonight?" Samson said loudly.

"Oh my, Samson can talk!" Anne, the receptionist, exclaimed.

"Oh, yes, Samson picks up words quite fast," Katy said. "We never know what Samson is going to say. I hope Samson hasn't offended you."

"Oh no, I am actually rather flattered," Anne, the receptionist, said, blushing in her cheeks. "I have never been asked out on a date by a cockatoo. He has really made my day!"

"Thank you again," Katy said.

"You are very welcome," Anne, the receptionist, answered.

"See you later, pretty lady! See you later, pretty lady!" Samson shouted as Father Williamson hurriedly pushed the cart toward the elevators. Everyone, including Anne, the receptionist, was laughing softly.

As they waited for the elevator doors to open, Katy bent down and said, "Chester, we will have a yummy snack after we visit Dave. There is a hamburger restaurant on the first floor. They have ice cream!" Chester immediately did his fancy twirl and made his chirpy sound and then softly meowed when he heard the word ice cream.

Did you hear that, Samson? We get ice cream! Ice cream is here! I scream, you scream, we all scream for ice cream! Chester said.

"Samson, cracker! Samson, cracker!" Samson squawked excitedly.

"Yes, Samson, there are crackers too," Katy said.

The elevator door opened, and everyone stepped inside.

"Ride! Ride! Whee!" Samson said as the elevator began to go up.

"Why do I have the feeling that Samson has been on an elevator before?" Father Williamson remarked. Katy and Mother Williamson giggled softly.

What is everyone giggling about? I don't see anything funny about what Samson is saying. That cockatoo is always trying to get all the attention. But I still love him. He is the best buddy a cat could have, Chester thought to himself.

Father Williamson pushed the button for the fifth floor. Everyone got off the elevator and started walking past the nurse's station. Suddenly, Nurse Betty shouted loudly, "Stop! Cats or birds are not allowed in this hospital!"

Chester immediately became upset and started twirling in circles, began to make a hissing noise, showed his teeth, and gave deep growls toward Nurse Betty. Samson became stressed, started screeching, and immediately said, "Trouble! Trouble! Help! Help! Save me! Save me!"

"It is all right, Chester and Samson," Katy said. "I will take care of this." Turning toward Nurse Betty, she said, "Please page Doctor Rufus."

"I will, and I already know what he is going to say!" said Nurse Betty as she stomped speedily to the phone. Father and Mother Williamson were shocked at the nurse's behavior toward them.

"I wonder how this is going to turn out," Father Williamson whispered in Mother Williamson's ear.

"I have no idea," Mother Williamson whispered back.

Katy was holding Chester in her arms, trying to keep him calm by petting him and rubbing his head. Father Williamson fed Samson a piece of cracker to keep him from becoming stressed. Samson's feathers were all fluffed out, and he continued to talk in between bites of the cracker. Crumbs of the cracker were falling on the hospital floor.

"Samson, are you all right? You sure are eating that cracker at a speedy rate. I know you are upset. I am upset too. I do not like loud noises. It alerts me to be on my guard when danger is near. I might have to attack. Be ready, ole buddy. This is not going to be pretty," said Chester. Chester's golden eyes were as big as golf balls, and he continued to hiss and growl. His tail was swishing back and forth speedily. Standing in a crouch position, Chester was ready to pounce on anyone who became a threat to his family. *"I will protect you, Samson. I am a Maine coon cat and I am very brave,"* Chester said. Samson tried to talk, but with all the pieces of cracker he had in his mouth and crumbs falling all over the hospital floor, only mumbling could be heard. No one could understand what Samson was trying to say. Samson's feathers were ruffled outward even more now, which made him look twice the size he actually was. Chester was frightened and stood behind Mother Williamson's legs, hoping he would become invisible. He feared what Samson was going to do next, being so stressed as he was. Katy covered her mouth with her hand, trying to hold back the laughter as she watched Samson.

"Paging Doctor Rufus to the fifth floor! Paging Doctor Rufus to the fifth floor immediately!" Nurse Betty said over the microphone.

Doctor Rufus got off a private elevator that doctors and nurses used. He walked up to the desk and asked, "Who paged me?"

"I did!" Nurse Betty answered. "This young lady has a cat and a bird in the hospital!"

"What is wrong with that?" Dr. Rufus asked.

"Well, I—" Nurse Betty began to say.

Doctor Rufus immediately interrupted Nurse Betty and said, "You show me where it says in our hospital policies, rules, and regulations that animals, birds, or even fish are not allowed in this hospital as long as they are on a leash, in a cage, or in an aquarium or fish bowl!" Dr. Rufus exclaimed. "Until then, you need to get to work, Nurse Betty!" He turned to Katy and said, "Katy, you may go in with Chester, Samson, and your parents."

"Thank you," Katy said in a humble, grateful voice.

"Thank you, Doctor Rufus," Father and Mother Williamson said.

Katy picked Chester up and placed him in her arms, trying to keep him calm. Samson gave a large squawk at Nurse Betty as they walked past the nurse's desk.

"Nurse Betty mean! Nurse Betty mean!" Samson said.

"Why I never!" Nurse Betty exclaimed.

Samson had turned around in his cage and stared at Nurse Betty, shaking his head sideways and back and forth wildly while Father Williamson walked as fast as he could, pushing the stainless steel cart that was holding the cage that Samson was in, down the hall to Dave's room so he could shut the door before Samson decided to say more words. Father Williamson had never seen Samson so upset and irritated. He feared what words Samson might say, being in one of the worst stress moods he had seen.

They entered Dave's room. "Before we begin, I feel it would be a good idea if everyone takes a deep breath in and lets it out slowly," Father Williamson suggested. Everyone, including Samson and Chester, took a deep breath and let it out slowly.

"That did help, Father. Thank you for that idea," Katy said. "That helped Samson quiet down." Katy walked up to the side of Dave's bed with Chester in her arms. "You remember Dave, don't you, Chester?" Katy said quietly. "Dave had an accident a few weeks ago. He is in a coma. That is when someone is asleep and won't wake up. I thought you would like to see Dave, and perhaps you could wake him or get him to respond in some way."

Chester was relaxed and purring with his ears standing straight up, listening to every word Katy was saying and looking at Dave at the same time.

Samson stood quietly inside his cage. His feathers were still fluffed outward, but as he watched Katy place Chester on Dave's bed, his feathers began to relax and were slowly folding back in place against his body.

"Here it goes," Katy said. Chester looked at Katy and then looked at Dave. He slowly walked closer to Dave and climbed on top of his stomach. He began pushing his paws up and down gently on Dave's stomach. He did this for two minutes. He then carefully lay on Dave's stomach, did his chirpy sound, meowed quietly, and began to purr. He remained on Dave's stomach for ten minutes. Chester slowly got up and began to lick Dave's right hand. He then moved close to Dave's face. He brushed up against his cheek with the left side of his body and walked to the top of his head. He made his chirpy sound several times and then walked to Dave's left side of his face and brushed against his cheek. Chester then walked to Dave's left hand and started licking it.

"Look!" Katy exclaimed. "Dave's hand is moving. He is touching Chester!"

Chester meowed softly while Dave caressed his body with his left hand.

"Chester," Dave said in a soft, sleepy voice. Dave opened his eyes.

"Hi, Dave," Katy said. "About time you woke up."

Dave looked up at Katy and smiled.

Father and Mother Williamson immediately went to the nurse's station to have Doctor Rufus paged. They noticed that Nurse Betty was no longer there.

"Where is the nurse that was here when we arrived?" Mother Williamson asked.

"She was excused from her schedule for the day," the nurse on duty answered.

"She didn't lose her job over that incident with the arrival of our cat and bird, did she?" Mother Williamson asked with a worried and concerned look on her face.

"No, Doctor Rufus thought it would be best if she took out some time and read the policies, rules, and regulations of the hospital," the nurse on duty answered. "When she comes to the part of animals, birds, and fish being allowed in the hospital, she is to write a written essay proving she understands. Doctor Rufus would never dismiss any of his nurses from their duties over a thing that happened earlier this morning. He is a wonderful, kind, and understanding doctor to work for."

"I am relieved," Mother Williamson said, giving a sigh. "Would you please page Doctor Rufus? Dave Middleton in room 508 has come out of his coma."

"That is wonderful to hear. I will do that right now!" the nurse on duty exclaimed.

Doctor Rufus walked into Dave's room. A nurse was taking Dave's blood pressure and temperature.

"Let me listen to your heart," Doctor Rufus said. "It is good to see you awake. Do you remember why you are in the hospital?" Doctor Rufus asked.

"No, not really," Dave said.

"Do you know the people standing in your room?" Doctor Rufus asked.

Dave looked at them and responded, "Katy, my wife, Mother and Father Williamson, Chester is sitting beside me, and there is Samson standing inside a cage on a stainless steel cart," Dave said.

"Samson cracker! Samson cracker! Dave awake! Dave awake!" squawked Samson.

"Follow the light with your eyes," Doctor Rufus said. "You did good with that. Are you hungry?" Doctor Rufus asked.

"Yes, and thirsty," Dave answered.

"I will let Katy tell you why you are in the hospital and have the nurse come in with water on ice and take your order," Doctor Rufus said.

"Oh, Dave, I am so relieved that you are awake," Katy said, giving him a kiss on his cheek.

"I will check on you later," Doctor Rufus said as he walked out of the room.

"Hi, I am Julie. I will be your nurse for the day. It is good to see you awake, Dave. What are you hungry for?" Nurse Julie asked.

"I would like a double cheeseburger with lettuce, mayo, dill pickles, onion, double order of french fries, chocolate malt, and a large piece of apple pie with a large scoop of vanilla ice cream."

Katy's eyes got big, like golf balls. "Oh my, you are hungry, Dave!" Katy exclaimed, giving a chuckle.

"I think you better start with some toast, soft egg and a small vanilla shake," Nurse Julie suggested. "If you keep that down, then we will go for that order you just made. May I get anyone else something?" Nurse Julie asked.

"Would you bring a small dish of vanilla ice cream with two spoons and some saltine crackers," Katy said.

"Sure!" Nurse Julie said.

"Oh boy! I know who that is for! Me! Me! Me! Yum, yum, yum! Samson, get ready! Ice cream is coming!" Chester said.

"Samson cracker! Samson cracker!"

While Dave ate, Katy told him what had happened. Dave was beginning to remember. "Did they catch the two men in the convenience store?" Dave asked.

"The last we heard, no," Father Williamson said.

"You have had a lot of visitors, Dave," Katy said.

"I see that by the looks of my room," Dave said. "Balloons, cards, flowers! Is that a box of assorted chocolates and a jar of cashews?" Dave asked.

"Yes, but you better wait on those too," Katy said.

"All right, take them home, and we can all enjoy them after I am released from the hospital," Dave said.

"Dave, do you remember where we had gone before you were shot at the convenience store?" Katy asked.

Dave looked at her with a puzzled look, trying to think. "I took you to Frankie and Johnnies for dinner, and then we went dancing at the ballroom. It was our first Valentine's celebration," Dave said.

"Dave, I love you so much," Katy said as she hugged him.

Chester was licking his ice cream from a spoon. *I'm not just a sheriff. I am now a nurse. I woke Dave up. Just call me Nurse Chester! Yup, that's me. Is there anybody else that needs to be woken up?* thought Chester as he licked the outside of his mouth.

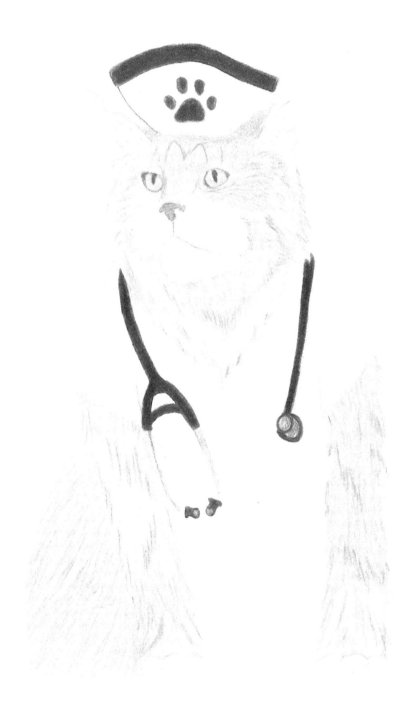

Chester looked upward and saw an object sitting on top of a chest of drawers. He jumped on top and was amazed when he looked at the object. *I am such a good-looking fella!* Chester thought as he stared at the picture, thinking it was him seeing himself in a mirror.

"Dave should rest now," Nurse Julie said. "Do come back and bring Chester and Samson too."

"Okay, thank you," Katy said. They said their goodbyes and told Dave to call if he felt lonely.

After arriving home, Katy called Pastor Mike and told him the good news that Dave had come out of his coma. Pastor Mike started a calling chain where he calls the first person, and that person calls the next on the list. Katy then called Scott and Peggy. They volunteered to call everyone who worked in Sweetwater. The news spread quickly. Katy's phone was constantly ringing. Friends wanted to tell her they were happy that Dave had awakened and was doing fine.

Dave had many visitors throughout the week and was able to return home within five days. He had strict orders from Doctor Rufus to stay home for two weeks so he could regain his strength.

Katy kept very busy keeping Dave entertained and making sure he followed his restrictions daily that Doctor Rufus had written down.

Many friends came to visit Dave while he was at home. Some of the farmers came and played checkers with him too, to help pass the time during his recovery. They also made sure the snow was shoveled from the front porch and sidewalk leading up to it. The front and back driveways were always kept clear.

Katy would show how grateful she was for all their friends and neighbors' kindness in helping by having a delicious meal waiting for them when they came.

Chapter 16

It was a gloomy, cloudy Monday in the middle of March. The logs were burning steadily from the fireplace in the sitting room. Dave and Katy were sitting in their wingback recliners, watching a movie on television. Chester was curled up in the circular tube of his cat condo, and Samson was sitting quietly on his wooden perch. Dave got up from his chair and looked out the window.

"The snow is almost gone," Dave remarked. "Spring will soon be here."

"I am really looking forward to spring arriving," Katy said. "It will be nice to sit on the enclosed porch again."

"Yes, Samson hasn't had a chance to enjoy the enclosed porch," Dave said. "He joined our little family after we closed the porch for the winter."

"Are you anxious to go back to work tomorrow?" Katy asked.

"Yes, I am," Dave answered joyfully. "It will be great seeing our steady customers come to the Garden and Landscape Store to purchase their garden and flower seed and supplies."

"Remember to take it slow and easy at first," Katy said. "You need to build your strength up. I don't want you to have a relapse and have to go back to the hospital."

"I will," Dave answered. "I plan to take breaks, and if I become tired, I will go to my office and rest awhile."

"That sounds like a good idea," Katy said, winking at Dave.

At eight o'clock in the morning, Ralph, the investigation team leader, walked toward his office.

"Joanie, do I have any messages?" Ralph asked.

"Yes, Tom wants to see you immediately in the screen room," Joanie replied.

"You know where I will be if you need me for anything," Ralph said as he walked away.

"Hi, Tom," Ralph said as he walked into the screen room that showed pictures of areas where the investigation team had set up surveillance cameras.

"Ralph, I am glad you are here," Tom said. "I think I have something that might be of interest to you." Tom started pushing buttons on a keyboard, and a picture came up on a large screen. "This is from the surveillance cameras that were set up outside and inside that pavilion belonging to Dave and Katy Middleton."

"Rather strange seeing two men wearing ski masks while they are inside playing a game of pool," Ralph said.

"I thought the same thing," Tom answered. "As you keep watching, they don't stay long. They play a game of pool, eat a sandwich, and they are on their way."

"Can you get sound so we can hear what they are saying?" Ralph asked.

"Sure!" Tom exclaimed as he pushed another button and turned a knob to the right.

"Start from the beginning when these two men arrive in their motorboat," Ralph said.

The surveillance cameras showed a man with a black ski mask over his face and a man with a blue ski mask over his face arriving in a motorboat at the cove outside the pavilion. The man with the black ski mask jumped out of the motorboat and wrapped a rope to the center of a tree located a few feet from the pavilion. The man with the blue ski mask jumped out of the motorboat and walked through the water of Cedar River and squeezed through the wall and glass doors standing on the concrete ledge. He began to unhook the left side of the large pressure-treated pine wall, and the man with the blue ski mask unhooked the right side of the large pressure-treated pine wall. As both men turned the cranks, the pressure-treated pine wall came down slowly and splashed on top of the water.

"Easy-peasy," said the man in the blue ski mask as he jumped on top of the large wooden plank. He slid the glass door open and pushed the black curtains to the side. Both men stepped inside. They began playing a game of pool and ate their sandwiches while speaking to each other.

"Hey, Mac, you think we will have any luck tonight catching that large goldfish we saw swimming in Cedar River?" the man with the black ski mask asked.

"I don't know, Roni," Mac answered. "We better wait till dark to check the trap we set early this morning. We don't want anyone seeing us."

"Yea, we sure don't want to get caught and have to pay a five-hundred-dollar fine," Roni said. "Are we staying at the stone cottage tonight?" Roni asked.

"Planning on it," Mac answered. "I left the logs burning in the fireplace so it will be toasty warm, and we can get a good night's sleep before moving on tomorrow morning. It's dark enough now. Let's be on our way."

"Thanks, Tom," Ralph said. "I want Sheriff Jesse to see this."

"Joanie, please give Sheriff Jesse a call," Ralph said as he walked toward his office. "I need to speak with him."

"Sure, Ralph," Joanie replied, picking up the phone receiver. "Ralph, I have Sheriff Jesse on line one," Joanie said over the intercom in Ralph's office.

"Thanks, Joanie," Ralph said as he pushed the line one button on his phone base.

"How are you doing, Sheriff Jesse?" Ralph asked.

"Great. Everything has been peaceful in Sweetwater for the past two weeks," Sheriff Jesse answered.

"I got some pictures that the surveillance cameras took at that underground pavilion belonging to Dave and Katy Middleton," Ralph said anxiously. "I thought you might be interested in coming over and taking a look at them."

"I am on my way," Sheriff Jesse said.

Sheriff Jesse arrived at the investigation building in Springfield, Oklahoma, within an hour. "Right this way, Sheriff," Ralph said, escorting him to the screen room.

"I am very impressed with how clear these pictures are," Sheriff Jesse said. "Too bad Mac and Roni don't take their ski masks off while they play a game of pool. I want Dave and Katy Middleton to see these pictures. Would you make a copy of these pictures so I can drop by the Middleton's home and let them go through them," Sheriff Jesse said. "They might know these two men from somewhere."

"Sure. Have your pictures in twenty minutes," Ralph said. "How about a cup of coffee?" Ralph asked.

"Sounds good. Thanks," Sheriff Jesse said as he followed Ralph to the lounge.

"Help yourself to a doughnut," Ralph said.

"Thanks!" Sheriff Jesse exclaimed as he reached for a vanilla crème-filled Bismarck with chocolate icing on top.

"Here are the photos you wanted," Joanie said, handing the folder to Ralph.

"Thanks, Joanie," Ralph said. "I need to be sure these photos are to your satisfaction," Ralph said as he pulled the pictures out of the folder and handed them to Sheriff Jesse.

"Even have a photo of their motorboat," Sheriff Jesse remarked as he looked through the pictures. "That motorboat has a name on the back of it."

"Yes, I noticed that too," Ralph said. "Some boats have names, and some have numbers and letters on the back of them."

"This one will be easy to remember," Sheriff Jesse said.

"Yes, the name Wild Kat would be easy to remember," Ralph said.

"Thanks for all your help, Ralph," Sheriff Jesse said as he got up from his chair and shook Ralph's hand.

"Keep in touch," Ralph said. "I am looking forward to hearing what the Middletons have to say after looking at the pictures."

"I will let you know," Sheriff Jesse said.

The phone was ringing in the sitting room as Katy and Chester were walking through the door. They had gone to buy groceries at Tony's Grocery Store in Sweetwater, Oklahoma. Katy quickly walked to the sitting room to answer the phone.

"Good afternoon, the Middletons," Katy said.

"Hi, Katy, this is Sheriff Jesse. I was wanting to know if I could stop by after five o'clock today?" Sheriff Jesse asked.

"Sure, Dave started back to work today," Katy said. "What is this visit about?" Katy asked.

"I have some pictures I want Dave and you to look at," Sheriff Jesse answered.

"Great!" Katy exclaimed. "I will give Dave a call and let him know."

"Thank you, Katy," Sheriff Jesse said. "See you and Dave shortly after five o'clock today."

"Dave and I will be waiting for your arrival," Katy said as she pushed the button down on the phone base to get a dial tone.

Katy immediately dialed the number of the Garden and Landscape Store.

"Garden and Landscape Store, this is Dave speaking."

"Hi, Dave, it's Katy. I just received a phone call from Sheriff Jesse. He wants to stop by after five o'clock today."

"What for?" Dave asked.

"He has pictures to show us," Katy answered.

"Pictures of what?" Dave asked.

"I assume pictures the surveillance cameras took inside and outside of the underground pavilion at the end of the concrete tunnel in our basement," Katy answered.

"Oh, I will try to get off before five o'clock," Dave said. "I will ask Scott to lock up."

"Okay, see you soon, sweetie," Katy said as she hung up the phone.

Dave drove back to the house at four-thirty in the afternoon. "I'm home, Katy!" Dave shouted as he walked into the kitchen.

"Hi, sweetie," Katy said, giving him a hug. "Sheriff Jesse should be here soon. I made a key lime pie and placed sliced cheddar cheese and an assortment of crackers on a tray for us to enjoy while we look at the pictures. The coffee is brewing."

"That was thoughtful of you, Katy," Dave said, giving her a kiss on the lips.

The bell on the front porch rang.

"I'll get that," Dave said as he rushed down the hall to open the front door. "Sheriff Jesse, come right in. Katy has coffee brewing in the kitchen."

"Dave, good to see you," Sheriff Jesse said as he shook Dave's hand. "I hear you started back to work today."

"Yes, it sure was good to get back on my daily schedule," Dave said.

"Have a seat at the table," Katy said as she placed the tray of cheese and crackers in the center. "Would you like a slice of key lime pie, Sheriff Jesse?" she asked.

"Yes, I sure would!" Sheriff Jesse exclaimed. "I haven't had key lime pie since I visited my parents last summer. Did you make this pie?" Sheriff Jesse asked.

"Yes, I did," Katy answered.

"It is delicious," Sheriff Jesse remarked.

"Help yourself to another piece if you like," Katy offered, handing the pie spatula to Sheriff Jesse.

"Don't mind if I do," Sheriff Jesse said as he placed another slice of the key lime pie on his plate. "I brought some pictures I would like you both to look at," Sheriff Jesse said as he opened the folder and placed the pictures in front of Dave and Katy. Dave and Katy began looking through the pictures and gasped when they came to the picture of the men wearing ski masks. "What is it?" Sheriff Jesse asked in a concerned voice.

"These are the two men in the convenience store on the morning in February who robbed money and shot a .22 caliber pistol in the air," Dave answered. "One of the bullets ricocheted from a shelf and hit me in the chest."

"Yes, you are right," Katy said. "I saw them run out of the convenience store and leave in their truck."

"Do you remember what make, model, and color the truck was?" Sheriff Jesse asked.

"It happened so fast, and when I saw Dave drop to the floor in the convenience store, my only concern was to get inside and help him," Katy answered.

"I understand," Sheriff Jesse said. "This is at a convenience store in Springville, Oklahoma. Am I correct?" Sheriff Jesse asked.

"Yes, if I remember correctly, it was called Hank's Quick Shop," Dave answered. "It was located along the highway just outside of Springville. We were on our way home from a night out, celebrating our first Valentine's Day together. We were at the convenience store at approximately two o'clock Saturday morning. Katy asked me to stop and pick up a quart of milk. She wanted to make pancakes for Scott and Peggy, who volunteered to watch Chester and Samson while we were gone."

"I am going to stop at that convenience store and find out the name of the cashier who was working that night," Sheriff Jesse said. "He might know something."

"I still can't figure out why there is a rowboat hidden among the trees when they have a motorboat," Dave said.

"They probably would use the rowboat if their motorboat wouldn't start," Sheriff Jesse said. "They wouldn't want to get stranded at the pavilion."

"I never thought of that," Dave said.

"Do you know the two men's names?" Katy asked.

"Yes, I have the names right here," Sheriff Jesse said. "The man with the blue ski mask is Mac, and the man with the black ski mask is Roni."

"That is easy to remember, Mac and Roni," Dave said, giving a chuckle.

"You are right. I never thought of it that way," Sheriff Jesse said, chuckling also.

"Keep in touch, Sheriff Jesse," Dave said.

"Thank you for the delicious pie and coffee," Sheriff Jesse said as he walked to his car.

"I would never have thought it would be the two men who robbed that convenience store in February," Dave said.

"It came as a shock to me too," Katy answered. "I hope it doesn't take too long to find out who they are and why they are coming to our pavilion."

"Stay away from that tunnel and pavilion, Katy," Dave said in a serious voice. "Keep that door padlocked under the oak stairway."

"I will," Katy answered. "I wish the door leading to the tunnel could also be padlocked," she said in a concerned voice.

"I will call Sheriff Jesse and ask if it is all right to do that," Dave said. "It would be double protection for us as we live in the house."

"I would feel better if we could do that," Katy said.

"It is a great idea, Katy," Dave said. "I will give Sheriff Jesse a call right now."

"We can eat in the sitting room and watch TV for a while," Katy said. "It has been a busy day for you, returning to work after your recovery and finding out it is the same two men in our pavilion that were in that convenience store. You need time to relax so you will sleep well."

"That would be great," Dave said as he dialed the number.

Katy carried the tray holding two bowls of ravioli and cheese, along with slices of homemade bread with butter, to the sitting room.

"Sheriff Jesse said it would be all right to padlock that door," Dave said. "He suggested placing a bolt lock on the door and an iron bar across the door also. That would be extra security for us while we live in our home."

"That is a wonderful idea!" Katy exclaimed. "I will definitely feel safer when that door won't open from the other side."

"To be honest, Katy, I will feel safer too," Dave said. "I will stop at the hardware store tomorrow and get a heavy padlock, bolt lock, and metal bar. I will try to install them when I get home tomorrow afternoon. When is Easter?" Dave asked.

"Easter Sunday is on April 25 this year," Katy answered.

"That is in three weeks," Dave said.

"I know. I should give Mother a call to see what their plans are," Katy said.

"You should do that right now," Dave said. "I have something to talk to you about after your phone call."

Katy dialed the number on the phone.

"The Williamsons!"

"Hi, Mother, it is Katy."

"Hi, Katy. How are you both doing?" Mother Williamson asked.

"Great!" Katy said. "Dave started back to work today."

"That is good news," Mother Williamson said.

"What do you and Father have planned for Easter?" Katy asked.

"Nothing much," Mother Williamson said. "We will probably attend sunrise services early in the morning and then church services after that."

"Would you and Father like to come here?" Katy asked with enthusiasm in her voice. "The Sugar Creek Lutheran Church has sunrise services along with a potluck breakfast before the church services. Father and you can eat Easter dinner with Dave and me. You are welcome to stay over if you like and stay as long as you want."

"Let me ask your father," Mother Williamson said.

"Sure! Sounds great!" Father Williamson said anxiously. "It will do us both good to get away, and there is no better place to be than Dave and Katy's home."

"Your Father is looking forward to it," Mother Williamson said. "Is there anything you would like me to bring?" Mother Williamson asked.

"No, Mother, I have everything handled, but thank you for offering," Katy said. "Dave and I are looking forward to seeing you both at Easter."

"We are looking forward to seeing you and Dave also," Mother Williamson said.

"Love you and take care," Katy said.

"Your father and I send our love to you and Dave too," Mother Williamson said. "Goodbye."

"Mother and Father are coming for Easter," Katy said.

"Great!" Dave said.

"What did you want to talk to me about?" Katy asked.

"Come sit beside me," Dave said.

"Okay," Katy said as she slid into her wingback recliner.

"Something happened, Katy, when I was in that coma," Dave said, looking very serious. "I want to tell you about it. I have not told anyone, not the nurses, not Doctor Rufus, not Mother and Father

Williamson or any of our friends. Not even Chester or Samson! You are the first to hear this."

"I am all ears, Dave. What is it you would like to tell me?" Katy asked.

"When I was in my coma, I was talking with someone. I have no idea who it was. This being stood tall and glistened with a light that was beautiful and very bright. It was difficult to look at it. It reminded me of an angel, one of God's messengers sent to speak to me."

"Oh my, Dave, this is very interesting," Katy said. "What did this messenger say?" Katy asked.

"The messenger being brought me back to the days where I was brought up in foster homes after my parents died in their car accident," Dave continued. "I was reminded how depressed I sometimes got knowing I didn't have a family like other children. The messenger being showed me many foster children going through the same feelings I had gone through. I remember asking, 'What am I to do?' The messenger being said these exact words, 'You, Dave, and your wife, Katy, have shown goodness caring for Chester, Samson, and all the animals and birds in Dark Woods. The fish and reptiles in and along Cedar River have also been cared for. You both go out of your way to help the people of Sweetwater, Oklahoma, and Katy's parents, John and Mary Williamson. Since you have no children of your own, you are to adopt a child from the Foster and Adoption Agency in Oklahoma City, Oklahoma.'" He then continued, "The next thing I knew, I was touching Chester, and I woke up from my coma. I remember seeing you beside my bed, and Samson was standing in a cage. Your parents were standing on the other side of my bed."

"Dave, how did you keep from telling me this before?" Katy asked.

"It has been going around in my mind ever since I woke up that day," Dave said. "At first, I thought it was a dream, but I can't stop thinking about it. Tell me what you think."

"I think we should look into this," Katy said. "An angel was sent to deliver a message to you while you were in your coma!" Katy exclaimed with great excitement. "Let me find the phone number and address of an adoption agency in Oklahoma City."

Katy opened the phone book, and there before her eyes was the page with the Foster Care and Adoption Agency listing.

"Oh my! I just opened the book, and voilà, here it is," Katy said.

"Yes, I see that," Dave said. "Go ahead and make the phone call, Katy."

"No, Dave, the messenger being spoke to you," Katy said with a grin on her face. "You make the phone call."

"Okay!" Dave said. "Stay sitting beside me while I talk to them. Write down notes as I talk."

"Okay, let me get a pen and a pad of paper," Katy said.

"Ready?" Dave asked.

"Yes, dial away," Katy said, giving a slight giggle.

"Foster Care and Adoption Agency, how may I help you?"

"Hi, this is Dave Middleton of Sweetwater, Oklahoma. My wife, Katy, and I have been thinking about adopting. Could you give me some information on what is involved in adopting?" Dave asked.

"Yes, I will be happy to help you with that," the receptionist said. "First, there is paperwork to be filled out. Second, we wait for a child needing to be adopted that meets your expectations. Third, a background check is made on you and your wife to be sure you meet the requirements to become parents of an adopted child. Fourth is the amount you will be responsible for paying for the adoption of a child. Would you like to make an appointment to come to our agency and discuss it?" asked the receptionist.

"Yes, what openings do you have?" Dave asked.

"I have a ten o'clock opening this coming Friday morning," the receptionist answered.

"Just one moment, please," Dave said. "Katy, are you free to meet with them at ten o'clock this Friday morning?" Dave asked.

"Yes, that works for me," Katy said anxiously.

"Yes, that would definitely work," Dave said to the receptionist.

"We will be looking forward to seeing you both at ten o'clock this coming Friday morning," the receptionist said.

"Thank you and have a wonderful day," Dave said.

"We have to remember it is a three-hour drive," Katy said.

"We should be able to leave by seven o'clock in the morning," Dave said. "We will drop Samson and Chester at the Garden and Landscape Store on our way. I am sure Scott won't mind watching them while I am away."

"That is a good idea," Katy said. "I am sure we will be back before Scott closes the store at five o'clock in the afternoon."

Chapter 17

At ten o'clock on Friday morning, Dave and Katy arrived at a large two-story brick building. On the front was a large sign that said, "Foster Care and Adoption Agency."

"This is the place," Katy said.

Dave and Katy walked through the double glass doors and stood in front of the receptionist's desk.

"Hi, I am Dave Middleton, and this is my wife, Katy," Dave said.

"It is very nice to meet you both," the receptionist said. "Tracy is expecting you. Have a seat, and I will let her know you both have arrived."

A young woman in her middle twenties came to the waiting room. "Hello, my name is Tracy," she said as she shook Dave's and Katy's hands. "I will be working with you to get you started on the foster care and adoption process. Please come with me to my office where we can talk in private."

As they walked into Tracy's office, they noticed many pictures of children hanging on the walls. "Please have a seat," Tracy said. "The first thing I want you to know is you will need to attend an orientation meeting. This is where you learn more about children in our foster care and adoption agency, the roles and responsibilities of adoptive and foster parents, the process you will need to go through to adopt or foster a child, next steps to be taken on your journey to adoption or becoming a foster parent. Are you still interested?" Tracy asked.

"Yes," Dave and Katy said together immediately.

"How do we attend an orientation meeting?" Dave asked.

"I will set that up for you," Tracy said. "Are you free anytime?" she asked.

"Yes, we will make it work no matter when it is scheduled," Dave said.

"That is great!" Tracy said. "That is the attitude I like to hear. You have already passed step one. I will call you and let you know when your orientation meeting is. Show up with an open heart and mind. Ask questions and listen carefully to what the presenters say. Take notes on things such as what you have to do next, who your important contacts are, and when the next meeting is scheduled. During your first orientation meeting, you may hear for the first time the real challenges involved in becoming a foster parent and adopting a child from the Foster Care and Adoption Agency in the state of Oklahoma. It is natural to have a strong disagreement or bad feelings as your emotions rise to the surface. You don't have to make any major decisions at this point. The only thing you need to do is decide whether you want to continue to explore becoming a foster care or adoptive parent. I will be in touch with you soon. It was very nice meeting you both. Have a nice day and a safe drive back to your home," Tracy concluded as she stood and shook Dave's and Katy's hands.

"Oh, Dave, I am so excited!" Katy said as they were driving back to the Garden and Landscape Store in Sweetwater to pick up Chester and Samson. "I feel like we should stop at Mother and Father's and say hi," Katy said. "We always do when we are shopping in Oklahoma City."

"In order to keep it quiet, we better not stop to see Mother and Father," Dave suggested. "Chester and Samson are waiting for us, and I would like to get back to Sweetwater before the work traffic becomes busy."

"Let's stop at Sammy's Sugar Shack and pick up some cheeseburgers, curly fries, and shakes for supper before we stop at the Garden and Landscape Store," Katy suggested.

"Sounds good to me," Dave said. "Remember, we need to keep this to ourselves, for now, Katy."

"I agree," Katy said. "My lips are sealed."

Chapter 18

The first week in April had gone by. Dave was getting ready to leave for work at the Garden and Landscape Store. As he bent down to place Samson on his shoulder, the phone rang.

"Good morning, the Middletons. This is Dave speaking."

"Hello, Dave. This is Tracy at the Foster Care and Adoption Agency in Oklahoma City."

"Hello, Tracy, how are you this beautiful April day?" Dave asked.

"I am doing very well," Tracy answered. "How are you and Katy?" Tracy asked.

"Katy and I have been anxious to hear from you," Dave said. "Katy, it is Tracy from the Foster Care and Adoption Agency!" Dave shouted with joy.

Katy dropped the breakfast plate she was washing back in the sink of water, wiped her hands quickly on a towel, and ran to the sitting room.

"Say hello to Tracy, honey," Dave said as he handed the phone receiver to Katy.

"Hello, Tracy, it is so good to hear from you," Katy said with excitement in her voice.

"I have a date for you and Dave to start your orientation meeting," Tracy said. "Would this Monday work?" Tracy asked.

"Dave, Tracy wants to know if this Monday will work for our first orientation meeting," Katy said.

"Yes! Yes! Be sure to find out what time," Dave exclaimed.

"Yes, Monday will work, Tracy," Katy answered. "What time?" Katy asked.

"The first meeting begins at two o'clock in the afternoon," Tracy answered. "It usually lasts three hours."

"Okay, Dave and I will be there on Monday at two o'clock sharp," Katy said. "Where is the meeting being held?" Katy asked.

"Come to the Foster Care and Adoption Agency in Oklahoma City," Tracy said. "There is an elevator you can take to the lower floor. That is where all the meetings will be held."

"Sounds fantastic. Dave and I will be there!" Katy said.

Katy then handed the phone receiver to Dave. "Hi, Tracy, I just have one question," Dave said. "Do you have any idea when the other meetings will be held?" Dave asked. "I want to be sure my assistant, Scott, can be in charge at the Garden and Landscape Store while I attend the meetings."

"I understand, and I am glad you asked," Tracy said. "You just passed step three."

"Really!" Dave said. "What was step two?" he asked.

"Answering the phone on the first ring when I called you," Tracy said, giggling softly. "The answer to your question is the other meetings will be held that same week at ten o'clock in the morning. Will all these scheduled days and times work for you and your wife, Katy?" Tracy asked.

"Yes, we will definitely be there," Dave said. "Thank you, and have a fantastic day."

"You and Katy do the same," Tracy responded.

"Katy, I have to leave for work," Dave said, giving Katy a big hug and a kiss. "I have to be sure Scott can work for me next week."

"Okay," said Katy. "What about Chester and Samson while we are attending the meetings next week?" Katy asked.

"Tomorrow is my Saturday off," Dave said. "I am going to try to switch with Scott and work. I will let you know what I have planned when I get home. Come on, Samson, time to go to work!" Dave said, looking around the sitting room for Samson.

The clickety-clack, clickety-clack sound of Samson's feet could be heard from the hall.

"Samson work! Samson work!" squawked Samson as he flew up to Dave's shoulder.

"Hi, boss," Scott said as Dave walked through the glass door of the Garden and Landscape Store. "Samson, how are you doing?" Scott asked.

"Samson work! Samson work!" Samson said as he flew off Dave's shoulder and walked to the room where the aquariums and cages of hamsters, guinea pigs, snakes, mice, and the one and only tarantula were. Samson flew to his wooden perch and started squawking loudly, "Howie out! Howie out! Trouble! Trouble! Help! Help! Squawk! Squawk! Danger near! Danger near!"

Dave and Scott immediately ran to the room, and sure enough, the large black fuzzy-wuzzy tarantula, Howie, had escaped from his aquarium. The wire-vented top had been slid open.

"Scott, there is Howie!" Dave exclaimed as he pointed to the tarantula walking slowly on the floor near the cat scratch posts. Scott carefully picked up Howie, the tarantula, and placed him back in his safe aquarium home. "We need to figure out a way to keep that wire-vented top from sliding," Dave said. "This could happen on a weekend or during the night when we are not here."

"I got an idea," Scott said. He walked quickly to the storage room and came back with four lightweight brackets. He attached the brackets to the top and bottom of the aquarium's four sides. "There, that should do it," Scott said. "Howie, our fuzzy-wuzzy black tarantula will be safe now."

"Great idea, Scott," Dave said.

"Howie safe! Howie safe!" squawked Samson as he folded his ruffled feathers close to his body and settled down.

"Here is a cracker, Samson," Dave said. "Thank you for alerting us about Howie."

"Mmmm! Cracker! Mmmm! Cracker!" Samson said as he chomped away, enjoying his cracker and watching the hamsters on their wheel going around and around and around. "Howie treat! Howie treat!" Samson squawked.

"Here you go, Howie," said Scott as he dropped two beetles into his aquarium to enjoy as his treat.

"Scott, I have a favor to ask," Dave said.

"I'm all ears," Scott said, chuckling.

"Since recuperating from the bullet being removed from my chest and working at the store daily, I was wanting to take a week off next week and go somewhere with Katy," Dave said. "I will work your Saturday morning tomorrow and—"

"Sure," Scott said immediately. "No problem. Where are you going?" Scott asked.

"Katy has always wanted to show me her apartment that she and Chester lived in and the Sunset Elementary School she taught music at in Oklahoma City," Dave said. "We want to have some leisure time together before the busy time of spring and summer arrive."

"Works for me," Scott said.

"Great and thank you, Scott," Dave said. "Katy says thank you too."

"No problem, Dave," Scott said. "I am glad you are well. You and Katy need some alone time together. There is plenty to see in Oklahoma City. I will write down some interesting places with their address if you like."

"That would be great!" Dave exclaimed. "List some great restaurants too."

"You got it, boss," Scott said, chuckling as he walked to the office.

Chapter 19

"Hi, Dave, how was your day?" Katy asked as she took Dave's coat and hung it up.

"Great, Katy," Dave answered. "I will be working tomorrow morning, and Scott will be able to work next week and Saturday morning."

"Fantastic," Katy said with a smile. "What about Chester and Samson?" she asked.

"I have an idea to present to you," Dave said.

"Sit down at the table. Supper is ready," Katy said as she placed a large pan of lasagna on the table and a bowl of crisp lettuce salad with radishes, cucumbers, and Italian dressing.

"Let me put Chester's and Samson's food in their bowls," Dave said. After saying grace, Dave took a bite of lasagna. "This is really delicious," Dave said.

"Don't forget to help yourself to the cheddar toast I made in the oven," Katy reminded him.

"Here is my plan," Dave said. "There are two options. Option one, have Mother and Father Williamson come and stay at our house with Chester and Samson. We can stay at a motel so we won't have to drive three hours every day to attend the meetings next week. Father Williamson can help Scott at the Garden and Landscape Store and take Samson with him. That way, Samson will stay on his regular schedule. Mother Williamson can keep Chester entertained. Option two," he paused, "we stay with Mother and Father at their home in Oklahoma City and let them know we are thinking about adopting a child. Chester and Samson can stay with Mother and Father while we attend our meetings. Now your turn, Katy," Dave said. "Tell me your thoughts on each option, and if you have another idea, share it with me."

"I don't have another idea," Katy said. "As for option two, I don't want Mother and Father to know that we are thinking about adopting. If we aren't accepted after the meetings, it will break their hearts. I like option one! I am sure Scott will appreciate having Father come to help at the Garden and Landscape Store. It is a busy time of the year, with Easter and spring coming up. It would probably be good for Mother and Father to get away also. There is no better place than our home for them to get away to. Seems like something exciting always happens when they stay at our home."

"All right, option one it is!" Dave exclaimed. "Now we need to call them and ask if they would like to come and stay at our home for a week."

"I will clean up the dishes while you take a shower," Katy said. "We will make the phone call together."

"Sounds great. See you in the sitting room," Dave said.

Katy came, walking into the sitting room with a tray of hot cocoa and oatmeal cookies. "Let me help you with that," Dave said as he took the tray from Katy and placed it on the table along the wall in the sitting room.

"I thought we could enjoy hot cocoa and cookies after the phone call," Katy said.

"That was very thoughtful of you," Dave said.

"Mother and Father should be finished with their supper," Katy said. "Would you like me to call them, or would you like to call them, Dave?" Katy asked.

"You call them, but I do want to talk to them after you are finished," Dave said.

Katy dialed the phone number.

"The Williamsons."

"Hi, Mother, it is Katy. How are you and Father?" Katy asked.

"We are fine," Mother Williamson said. "We are counting the days for Easter and spring to arrive."

"Don't forget our plans for Easter," Katy said.

"I have it marked on the calendar," Mother Williamson said.

"Mother, Dave and I have a favor to ask of you," Katy said.

"Yes, what is it?" Mother Williamson asked.

"Dave and I were wanting to get away for a week, in fact, next week to be exact," Katy said. "We were wanting to know if Father and you would like to stay at our home and take care of Chester and Samson. Scott sure could use some help at the Garden and Landscape Store with Easter and spring just around the corner."

"Where are you planning to go?" Mother Williamson asked.

"I have never shown Dave the apartment Chester and I lived in and the school I taught music at before moving to Sweetwater," Katy said.

"Where would you be staying?" Mother Williamson asked.

"There are many motels to choose from," Katy said.

"I won't have that, Katy Middleton," Mother Williamson said in a stern voice. "If your father and I are staying at your home, you will be staying at ours!"

"That is nice of you, Mother," Katy said.

"That is the only way your father and I will do this," Mother Williamson added. "Let me ask your father." Then she said, "John, Dave and Katy want us to stay at their home next week so they can get away for a while."

"Sounds good to me," Father Williamson answered.

"Your father agrees," Mother Williamson said. "When do you want us to come?" Mother Williamson asked.

"If you come sometime tomorrow, we can go to church together on Sunday," Katy said. "After lunch, Dave and I will leave."

"I think it would be best if we will meet you at the Sugar Creek Lutheran Church Sunday morning," Mother Williamson said. "See you soon!"

"Don't hang up, Mother. Dave wants to talk to you," Katy said as she handed the phone receiver to Dave.

"Hi, Mother, I wanted to thank you," Dave said. "I really appreciate this on such short notice."

"You are welcome," Mother Williamson replied. "It will do your father and I some good to get away too. There is nothing like the country. It has been a long, drawn-out winter. Not much to do until spring arrives."

"Love you, Mother," Dave said.

"We love both of you too," Mother Williamson said. "See you tomorrow morning."

"Let's have cocoa and cookies," Dave said.

"I am so happy!" Katy exclaimed.

Chapter 20

Dave, Katy, and Chester had arrived at the Sugar Creek Lutheran Church at nine o'clock in the morning. Upon their arrival, Jim ushered Mother and Father Williamson to the second row from the front, where Dave, Katy, and Chester were sitting. After the church service, they all returned to the yellow Victorian house and ate a delicious lunch that Katy had prepared. During the afternoon, they visited for a while. Father and Mother Williamson suggested places for Dave and Katy to visit while staying at their home in Oklahoma City.

"You must go see the Barrels of the Oklahoma City Underground," Father Williamson said. "It covers over twenty city blocks filled with art and history exhibits. It doesn't have just one entrance. Oh no, there are many secret entrances scattered throughout downtown."

"Don't forget the Myriad Botanical Gardens," Mother Williamson said. "Fifteen acres of landscape with plants from all parts of the globe."

"Dave, I know you will enjoy seeing the Cowboy and Western Heritage Museum," Father Williamson remarked excitedly. "There are American Indian and Western artifacts from firearms to saddlery and Native American art. And then be sure to go to Frontier City. It is Oklahoma's only theme park, and there is a double Ferris wheel. You know, Katy's favorite ride at the theme parks is the Ferris wheel, Dave. Have you been on a double Ferris wheel, Katy?" he asked.

"No, I have not," Katy said, smiling.

"This would be your chance to do that," Father Williamson said, smiling in return. "You can walk through a haunted mine and a replica of a western town and watch staged robberies. There is even a saloon you and Katy can go in and order one of their fruity sizzle drinks."

"It is a beautiful sight to visit Bricktown," Mother Williamson said. "It has many boutiques and vintage stores to visit. You know, Dave, how much Katy likes to go shopping. Be sure to take the water taxi down the canal. It is so romantic!" Mother Williamson exclaimed, giving a wink.

"There are two museums you can visit," Father Williamson said. "The Museum of Osteology, which is America's only skeleton museum of creatures great and small. Then there is the Science Museum that is next door to the zoo. It is 30,000 square feet and is the one and only interactive science museum. It has everything from dinosaur skeletons to the world-class Kirkpatrick Planetarium. Don't forget the Oklahoma Zoo, which sits on 119 acres of land and is right next door. Be sure to stop and visit all the animals, including the giraffes, camels, and rhinos. There are walking trails to enjoy also."

"There is the Arcadia Lake on the Deep Fork River," Mother Williamson said. "You can have a waterside barbeque, and there is the Storybook Forest nearby you can walk through. The most beautiful park to visit is the Will Rogers Park. It is located at 3400 Northwest Thirty-Sixth Street. It is so beautiful and peaceful! You can really absorb the natural beauty on thirty acres of land. The beautiful landscapes and gardens offer a wide variety of trees, shrubs, and flowers. Most trees are labeled just in case you want to know what kind of tree it is. A creek or small stream runs through the park, and you will see orange fish, turtles, geese, ducks, and squirrels. Hidden throughout the park are fairy and gnome houses. There is a cactus viewing area, rose gardens and other flowering gardens, walkways, an arboretum, and an educational center."

"Be sure to take your camera. It is a great place to take pictures!" Father Williamson exclaimed. "Really take notice how large the Will Rogers Park is. You might want to buy thirty acres of land someday and do something similar as a tourist attraction for Sweetwater, Oklahoma."

"I never thought about that," Dave said.

Dave and Katy left for Oklahoma City at four o'clock in the afternoon. They drove into Mother and Father Williamson's garage at half-past seven in the evening. Dave carried the luggage into the house while Katy started placing items in the dresser of the spare bedroom.

"I am tired after driving for three hours," Dave said.

"I am quite tired myself," Katy said. "We need to get a good night's sleep before our first meeting at the Foster Care and Adoption Agency tomorrow."

"I agree. Let's call it a day," Dave said.

Back at the yellow Victorian house, Mother and Father Williamson had just finished watching the news on TV.

"I am tired, John," Mother Williamson said as she got up from her recliner in the sitting room.

"I am right behind you," Father Williamson replied.

I think I will sleep upstairs tonight, Chester thought as he followed Mother and Father Williamson up the spiral stairway. *Ahhhh! The window is open. I am so happy. The night is still, and there is a full moon. It will be easy to see anything moving about our yard and hear any sound made*, Chester thought. Chester jumped on the window sill and peered out. *Well, nothing exciting is happening tonight.*

Chester thought as he jumped from the window sill and onto the bed, where he curled up beside Mother Williamson.

All of a sudden, Chester awoke with a startle, hearing a familiar noise.

"Ack! Ack! Ack! Wooo! Wooo! Ack! Ack!" Chester scurried off the bed and jumped on the window sill. He peered out, and there in the yard was Foxy Gent.

"Hi, Chester," Foxy Gent said.

"I am so glad to see you," Chester said.

"It was quite a winter. I am glad spring will soon be here," Foxy Gent said. "We need to meet, Chester."

"Didn't we plan this a year ago and that was when you didn't show up?" Chester asked in a disgusted meow.

"Yes, but I will be sure to be here this time, I promise," Foxy Gent said.

"What's the occasion?" Chester asked.

"Oh, thought we could go for a stroll through Dark Woods," Foxy Gent said. "Hadn't seen you since Christmas Eve when you helped all of us decorate that evergreen tree so Santa knew where to place his sleigh with all our gifts."

"All right, I will try to get out of the house at dusk. If it is raining, we will have to plan for another time," Chester said.

"Okay, see you at dusk unless it is raining," Foxy Gent said.

Chester knew he wouldn't have a problem waking up at dusk. Mother Williamson was an early riser.

Chapter 21

Monday at Sweetwater, Oklahoma

Chester awoke, smelling the aroma of coffee being made. He used his litter box and sharpened his claws on the scratch post. He scurried down the spiral stairway and ran down the hall to the kitchen. Samson was already eating his bird seed out of his bowl.

"Why, Chester, you are up early today," Mother Williamson said. "I will get your breakfast and a bowl of fresh water." Chester gobbled down the egg and cheese bits in white sauce, lapped some water, and then gave out his chirpy meow. He ran to the front door and started twirling around and then stopped and looked at the door. "Do you want to go outside, Chester?" Mother Williamson asked. Chester gave out a loud chirpy meow. Mother Williamson opened the door, and Chester ran out. He hurried down the porch steps and ran toward the big oak tree. There standing by the oak tree was Foxy Gent waiting patiently.

"Chester, it is so good to see you," Foxy Gent said excitedly.

"It is good to see you too, Foxy Gent," Chester said.

"Jump on, Chester," Foxy Gent said. "I have something to show you."

Chester jumped on Foxy Gent's back, and away they went through Dark Woods. They traveled along Cedar River and came to Hoot Owl's tree.

After fifteen minutes…

"Whoooooo goes there?" Hoot Owl asked.

"Foxy Gent and Chester," Foxy Gent answered.

"Whaaat brings you here?" Hoot Owl asked. "I have not called a meeting."

"Something strange is going on across Cedar River," Foxy Gent said. "The small stone cottage has lights on, and smoke is coming from the chimney."

"Probably hunters," Hoot Owl said.

"Hoot Owl, it will soon be spring," Foxy Gent replied in a kind manner. "This is not hunting season."

"Ohhh! Sooo it is!" Hoot owl said, ruffling his feathers. "Well, all right then, gather everyone, and we will have a meeting. Be here by midmorning."

Foxy Gent and Chester scurried through Dark Woods and alerted all the animals, spiders, birds, rodents, reptiles, and insects of Dark Woods to meet at Hoot Owl's tree for an important meeting. Even the turtles had arrived on time.

At ten o'clock in the morning, Hoot Owl was standing outside his tree and announced, "Something strange is going on across Cedar River. The stone cottage has a flickering light inside, and smoke is coming out of the chimney. You all know the stone cottage has not been used for years by anyone, and now it seems it has been occupied by someone. The question is, 'Whooo?' We all must stay alert and keep a close eye on anything strange going on at that stone cottage. All agree say, 'Aye!'"

Everyone shouted, "Aye!"

"Hoot Owl, as everyone knows, I can't always be in Dark Woods because my home is with Dave and Katy, just west of here. But I will keep my ears perked if I hear anyone say anything about the stone cottage across Cedar River. If I hear anything, I will let you know right away," Chester said.

"Thank youuu, Chester," Hoot Owl said. "Youuu go to town now and then, don't youuu?" Hoot Owl asked.

"Yes, I do. Dave and Katy are out of town right now, but my grammy and grampy Williamson are staying at the house. I might be able to go with Grampy to the Garden and Landscape Store during the week. I will keep my ears perked up on any gossip swarming around town," Chester said.

114

"That would be great," Hoot Owl said. "Foxy Gent, you check with Chester now and then to see if he has heard anything."

"I will do that," Foxy Gent answered.

Everyone went about their business after the meeting. Chester decided to check out the lilac bushes in Dark Woods along Cedar River, hoping to see Trudie Butterfly. But instead, he saw a bird he had never seen before. It was completely black in color.

"Caw! Caw!" the bird said when it saw Chester.

"Who are you?" Chester asked.

"I am Calli Crow," the blackbird answered. "I live across Cedar River in a stone cottage. Who are you?" Calli Crow asked.

"I am Chester, a Maine coon cat. I am looking for Trudie Butterfly," Chester said.

"Kind of early for butterflies, isn't it?" Calli Crow remarked, looking strange at Chester.

"Yes, but I thought it wouldn't hurt to check," Chester said.

"Where do you live?" Calli Crow asked.

"Here, there, everywhere!" Chester answered.

"What do you do?" Calli Crow asked.

"This, that, everything!" Chester answered.

"You sure aren't much of a conversationalist, are you?" Callie Crow exclaimed.

"No, not really," Chester answered.

"Well, I'll best be going. Nice meeting you," Callie Crow said as she flew toward the direction where the stone cottage was sitting. The door of the stone cottage opened, and Calli Crow walked inside. Chester waited patiently to see if anyone else walked in or walked out of the stone cottage. Chester looked up to the sky and saw the sun was directly above him. He knew it was time for lunch. He scampered across the meadows and pathways of Dark Woods toward his home. There waiting for him was a bowl of chicken and gravy and a bowl of cool water in front of his white cupboard in the kitchen. After finishing his lunch, he curled up in his cat bed in the sitting room for an afternoon nap.

Chapter 22

Monday at Oklahoma City, Oklahoma

The alarm went off at six o'clock in the morning. Dave and Katy got up and had a light breakfast, which consisted of toast with butter and grape jelly. They each had a glass of orange/mango juice and coffee.

"Since the meeting doesn't start till two o'clock this afternoon, I thought we could drive to the apartment that Chester and I lived in and the Sunset Elementary School I taught music at," Katy suggested.

"That's a great idea," Dave said.

"I want to watch the weather first. I thought it would be nice to have our lunch in the park," Katy said.

"That would be nice," Dave said. "There is a restaurant that makes different kinds of sub sandwiches. They even include a choice of cookies and chips."

"Sounds good to me," Katy said as she cleared the dishes from the kitchen counter.

Two o'clock finally arrived. Dave and Katy stepped off the elevator to the lower floor of the Foster Care and Adoption Agency.

"Dave, look at all the people," Katy said. "There must be twenty-five couples here wanting to become foster parents or adopt a child."

"Glad you made it," said Tracy as she walked up to Dave and Katy. "Sign in on this paper and find a table to sit at. The presentation will begin shortly."

"Thank you," Dave and Katy said together. Dave and Katy walked to a table with two chairs in the front row and sat down.

"Don't get negative thoughts, Katy," Dave said. "There are many children waiting to be adopted. We need to stay positive."

"You are right," Katy said with a grin.

"Good morning, everyone! I will be your leader at all the meetings this week. My name is Kevin, and this is Tracy, whom all of you have already met. She will be in and out throughout our meetings this week. Let's begin by introducing yourselves and why you are wanting to become a foster parent or want to adopt a child."

Dave and Katy were last to introduce themselves.

"Hi, I am Dave Middleton, and this is my wife, Katy. Katy and I have been married for six months. We live in a three-story Victorian home with a Maine coon cat named Chester and a cockatoo named Samson. We have decided to adopt a child instead of having a family of our own. I, being a foster child myself, had always wondered what it would be like to have a family. I want to fill that empty space in a child's life that may be wondering the same thing. Talking it over with my wife, Katy, we agreed to adopt a child needing a home and a family through their growing up years."

"Thank you for introducing yourselves and sharing why you want to be a foster parent or would like to adopt a child," Kevin said. "Let's get started! Tracy will be handing out a quiz for you to take as a couple. You have fifteen minutes to complete the quiz."

After fifteen minutes…

"Time is up," Kevin announced. "Tracy will pick up the quizzes. While she is doing that, I will give my presentation."

"I want each of you to do the following. Envision what you want your family to be. You must keep an open mind. Learn about the children in foster care. Research financial and other supports that are available. Let's break these down so you will understand them better. Keep an open mind when entering your child's search. Review the children's stories. Ask your caseworker about the child's history and future needs. Your adopted child might not be the one you set out to find. Financial support is given to children with special needs. Some of the factors or qualifications for a special-needs child are being an older child, having a particular racial or ethnic background, being part of a sibling group needing to be placed as one unit, having medical conditions, having mental, physical, or emotional disabilities. If you are interested in adopting a child with special needs, ongoing monthly subsidies may be available to help with expenses after the adoption. Be sure to ask your child's caseworker if adoption subsidies are available. Now let's talk about adopting siblings. Many children are separated from their siblings because caseworkers were unable to find a permanent placement for all the children. Research has proven that siblings placed together experience a lower risk of failed placements, fewer moves, and many emotional benefits. Siblings placed together often feel more secure and are able to help each other adjust to their new family community. The next topic is adopting older children. To an older child in foster care, waiting for an adoptive family can feel like waiting for a miracle. You could be that miracle! Another option is adopting children of a different race or ethnicity. There is the option of adopting outside of the state you live in. Each one of you has a lot to think about. This is the end of our first session. If you still want to continue with the process of becoming a foster parent or adopting a child, please be here at ten o'clock tomorrow morning. I will present the process of getting approved to foster a child or adopt a child. On your way out, please pick up a paper that states Oklahoma's foster care and adoption guidelines at the front table. See you tomorrow!"

"That was very interesting," Katy said as Dave unlocked the door to Mother and Father Williamson's home.

"Yes, it sure was," Dave said. "It sure hit my heart when Kevin brought up that we could be someone's miracle which has been waiting for an adoptive family to take them in. I know that feeling, Katy."

"I am sure you do, Dave," Katy said. "That is probably why the messenger being spoke with you while you were in a coma."

"Would you like to order some fish for supper tonight?" Dave asked.

"Sure, there is a good fish restaurant called Poppy's Seafood," Katy said. "I will call in the order. While we eat, we can go over the Oklahoma foster care and adoption guidelines."

"That's a good idea," Dave said.

Later, the bell at the front door rang. "Order for Katy Middleton from Poppy's Seafood."

"Here is what we owe, and thank you," Dave said.

"I have never eaten fish and shrimp at Poppy's Seafood Restaurant," Katy said.

"It is really delicious. I like the cabbage coleslaw and rolls too," Dave said.

"Here are the licensing requirements for foster care or adoption," Katy said.

"What are they?" Dave asked.

"Must be at least twenty-one years old, must be in reasonably good health, may be single, married, divorced, or widowed, must have or provide sufficient beds and space for personal items for additional children, must be able to manage your income to meet the financial needs of your family, be capable, understanding, loving and accepting a child, provide protection and nurturance to the child/ children in your care, and act as a role model," Katy said.

"I think we have all that covered as a couple," Dave said.

"Yes, I agree," Katy said.

"Here is what we must complete on the home assessment," Dave said. "Completion of Oklahoma Department of Human Services forms and application, reference and background checks, medical examination report, fingerprinting, family assessment, which includes interviews with all family members, completion of a twenty-seven-hour resource family orientation, house safety assessment, verification of income sufficient to meet your needs, verification of vaccination for pets, automobile insurance verification. The forms and application will be filled out at one of our meetings."

"You and I are the only family members to be interviewed and complete a twenty-seven-hour resource family orientation," Katy said. "If anything needs to be done to the house for safety reasons, we definitely will get it done if told to do so."

"Chester and Samson have had their vaccinations," Dave said.

"The automobiles are insured. References, background checks, medical exam reports, and fingerprinting can be done when we are told to do so," Katy said.

"I am ready for our meeting tomorrow," Dave said. "How about you?" Dave asked.

"I am ready too," Katy said.

Chapter 23

Tuesday at Oklahoma City, Oklahoma

"Welcome back to the Foster Care and Adoption Agency," Kevin said. "This is your second day of our five meetings. It is good to see everyone has returned. Tracy has checked your quizzes and written down your scores in her book. Everyone did well. We will go over the quiz today. Another quiz will be given on Friday. These quizzes are given to show us how knowledgeable you were before the first presentation was given and how knowledgeable you have become when we meet on the last day of our meetings. Note that this does not stop you from being a foster parent or adopting a child from our agency. It is what I like to call food for thought! By Friday, when you take the other quiz, you will see how knowledgeable you have become by attending the meetings this week.

"Let's start with question one. Children enter foster care through no fault of their own, usually because their birth parents have struggled to keep them safe and healthy. Most come into care due to. The correct answer is neglect. The primary difference between foster care and adoption is that children are in. The correct answer is foster care temporarily. In the United States, the average age of children waiting to be adopted is age. The correct answer is eight. It typically takes. The correct answer is six to twelve months to be approved to adopt a child. All children removed from their families have experienced some form of. The correct answer is trauma. People who can be considered as foster care or adoptive parents must. The correct answer is be stable and mature. Successful and adoptive parents know that. The correct answer is they should seek out support and information.

While it is important to make a child feel like part of the family, foster care and adoptive parents must first. The correct answer is learn about and embrace the child's traditions, cultures, and individual preferences. When adopting from foster care, it is almost always better for children to have some. The correct answer is connection to their birth family. A foster or adoptive parent can best support a child who has been in care by. The correct answer is practicing trauma-informed parenting.

"Are there any questions or thoughts you want to share?" Kevin asked. "Okay, let's continue then. The first topic is getting approved," Kevin said. "The process of getting approved to foster and adopt are very similar. Many states give the option to families applying to adopt to also become licensed to foster. This is called a dual licensing process. Today, you will be completing an application. This is where you will be meeting with your caseworker, who will help you through the application process. Here are five things I want you to remember. Be open and honest on the application and during the personal interviews. Supply the necessary information completely, accurately, and timely. Ask for help if you don't understand something. Agree to maintain confidentiality about children in care and their birth families. Cooperate with the home inspection, criminal background, and protective service checks.

"If you have any concerns that might disqualify you from becoming a foster care or adoption parent, talk to your caseworker about it. If your caseworker finds you to be deceptive or dishonest or if documents are collected during the home study process exposing inconsistencies, the agency may not approve your application.

"Be prepared to provide or consent to the following: letters of reference from your employer and those who know you, criminal record check at local, state, and federal levels, proof of meeting the age requirement in your state, and verification of income to meet your expenses.

"Please keep in mind that you do not have to be rich to foster or adopt. Most adoptions from foster care are free, and any minimal fees associated with it are often reimbursable. Everyone will be assigned a caseworker today. The application must be completed and turned in tomorrow, which is Wednesday. If everything is filled out correctly on your application, you will then begin your preservice training. As I call out your name, please stand, and your caseworker will come to your table and escort you to their office." He paused. "Are there any questions?" Kevin asked. "Okay, I will see you tomorrow at ten o'clock in the morning. Have a wonderful day!"

"Dave, who are we going to contact for a letter of reference?" Katy asked. "We wanted to keep it quiet from everyone in Sweetwater."

"I thought about Dr. Rufus at the Methodist Hospital in Springville and Pastor Mike of Sugar Creek Lutheran Church," Dave answered. "We will explain to them that we want to keep it quiet. I am sure they will keep it confidential."

"That is a great idea," Katy said. "We will make the phone calls this evening."

"What about an employer?" Katy asked. "You are self-employed at the Garden and Landscape Store, and I haven't been employed since I resigned being a music teacher at the Sunset Elementary School in Oklahoma City."

"Do you know if the principal you worked under is still working at Sunset Elementary School?" Dave asked.

"No, but I could call the office and ask the secretary after we get home," Katy said.

"Let's stop and order a pizza," Dave said. "We will eat it at home and then make our phone calls."

"That is a splendid idea!" Katy remarked.

"You call Sunset Elementary first," Dave said.

"Okay," Katy said as she dialed the number on the phone.

"Sunset Elementary, this is Janice speaking. How may I help you?" Janice asked.

"Hi, this is Katy Middleton, and I was wanting to know who the principal is at your school."

"It is Principal Brown. Would you like me to connect you with him?" Janice asked. "He is in his office."

"Yes, please," Katy said.

"This is Principal Brown. How may I help you on this beautiful sunny day?" he asked.

"Hi, Principal Brown. I don't know if you remember me. My name is Katy Middleton. I was a music teacher at Sunset Elementary for several years under the name of Katy Williamson."

"Katy, I definitely remember you," Principal Brown said. "How have you been?" he asked.

"I am doing great, and how have you been?" Katy asked.

"Fabulous. Looking forward to warm weather," Principal Brown answered.

"I have a favor to ask of you," Katy said. "My husband, Dave, and I are wanting to adopt a child from the Foster Care and Adoption Agency in Oklahoma City. Would you be willing to write a letter of recommendation for me?"

"I will be pleased to do that," Principal Brown said. "Let me get a pen and paper so I can write down the Foster Care and Adoption Agency address."

"Okay, I am ready."

"What is their address?" Principal Brown asked.

"It's 5114 Lincoln Street, Oklahoma City, Oklahoma," Katy answered.

"I know where that agency is," Principal Brown said. "Instead of mailing it, I will deliver it to the agency in person. I will have it there by Friday of this week."

"Thank you, Principal Brown," Katy said. "I am very grateful for this."

"Happy to do it," Principal Brown said. "If you decide to teach music in the future, keep Sunset Elementary in mind. Take Care!"

"I will do that, Principal Brown," Katy said. "Thank you again, and have a wonderful day."

"My turn," Dave said as he dialed Pastor Mike's phone number.

"Good evening. This is Pastor Mike of the Sugar Creek Lutheran Church in Sweetwater, Oklahoma."

"Hi, Pastor Mike. This is Dave Middleton."

"Dave, it is good to hear from you," Pastor Mike said with a joyful voice. "How is everyone?" he asked.

"Katy and I are doing fine," Dave answered. "Chester and Samson are doing fine too. Everyone is looking forward to spring."

"Don't forget Easter sunrise services and that delicious breakfast potluck afterward in a couple of weeks," Pastor Mike said.

"We haven't forgotten," Dave said. "Mother and Father Williamson will be attending the services also."

"Fantastic! I look forward to seeing them," Pastor Mike said.

"Pastor Mike, Katy and I have a favor to ask of you," Dave said. "We want to adopt a child from the Foster Care and Adoption Agency in Oklahoma City. Would you be willing to write a letter of recommendation for us?" Dave asked.

"I would be pleased to do that," Pastor Mike said. "So many children are in need of a home to call their own. It is wonderful that you and Katy have decided to become parents of an adopted child. I will be going to the hospital in Oklahoma City tomorrow afternoon. Fred Brown fell on the ice while feeding his cattle this past Monday. Remember the sledding party was held at his farm in January."

"Yes, how is he doing?" Dave asked.

"It was a bad break, but you know Fred, a broken leg isn't going to keep him down," Pastor Mike said. "Several men have been helping with chores at the farm."

"Are his wife and children doing all right?" Dave asked.

"Yes, food is being brought in, and the teenagers of Sweetwater have offered to stay with the children so Fran can go visit Fred at the hospital daily," Pastor Mike said. "It's a three-hour drive, you know, so Fred doesn't get much company from Sweetwater with everyone having jobs and getting their children off to school. I have been going every day to keep him company."

"Katy and I will stop in to see Fred at the hospital after our meeting tomorrow," Dave said.

"I am sure he would like that," Pastor Mike said. "He loves to play checkers, and his favorite snacks are cashews and chocolate cordial cherries."

"Katy and I will help out at the Brown's farm after we return home," Dave said. "Our last meeting at the Foster Care and Adoption Agency is this Friday. We plan to drive home after that meeting."

"That is very thoughtful of both of you," Pastor Mike said.

"Pastor Mike, Katy and I would like the adoption we are considering to stay anonymous for now in case it doesn't work out," Dave said.

"No problem, Dave. I fully understand," Pastor Mike said. "This is Katy's and your joy to share with everyone when it is time."

"Thank you, Pastor Mike," Dave said. "Take care!"

"You and Katy take care too," Pastor Mike said. "I will be praying for both of you that your wish to adopt is accepted and that you will soon be parents of an adopted child."

"One more call," Dave said.

"Methodist Hospital, whom may I transfer your call to?" the receptionist asked.

"Doctor Rufus, please," Dave said.

"Who may I say is calling?" the receptionist asked.

"Dave Middleton," Dave answered in a pleasing voice.

"This is Doctor Rufus. How may I help you?"

"Hi, Doctor Rufus. This is Dave Middleton."

"Dave, how is everything going?" Doctor Rufus asked. "Hope all is well after your surgery."

"Yes, I am feeling great!" Dave exclaimed. "Doctor Rufus, the reason I am calling is my wife, Katy, and I are wanting to adopt a child through the Foster Care and Adoption Agency in Oklahoma City. We need a letter of recommendation. Would you be willing to write a letter on our behalf and send it to the agency for us?" Dave asked.

"Yes, of course, I will get that done immediately and get it in the mail today," Doctor Rufus answered. "I think it is wonderful what Katy and you have decided to do. Is there anything else I can help you with?" Dr. Rufus asked.

"No, that is all, and thank you for your time," Dave said.

"You are welcome, and take care," Doctor Rufus said.

"We have our three letters of recommendations, Katy," Dave said.

"That is wonderful," Katy said. "Let's take it easy and watch television before going to bed."

"Sounds good to me," Dave said.

Chapter 24

Tuesday at Sweetwater, Oklahoma

Chester and Samson had just finished eating their breakfast. Father Williamson was putting his coat on.

"Come on, Samson. We need to go to the Garden and Landscape Store to help Scott today," Father Williamson said.

"Chester and I are coming to the store today also," Mother Williamson said. "I want to get some ideas on what to plant in Katy's flower garden at the back of the house."

"That sounds like a great idea," Father Williamson said. "I will take Dave's truck to work so you can drive our car when you are ready to leave."

"Thank you, John," Mother Williamson said, giving him a hug goodbye.

"If you come close to noon, I will take you to lunch at Sammy's Sugar Shack," Father Williamson said.

"It's a date," Mother Williamson said, smiling.

Chester heard his grammy and grampy talking.

This is my chance to see if there is anyone who might know what is going on at that stone cottage across Cedar River, Chester thought. Chester heard Grampy call for Samson and watched them walk out the door.

A few hours later, Chester heard Grammy shout, "Chester, ride!"

Chester instantly ran to his white cupboard and got his collar. Grammy placed his collar around his neck, got his black leash, and they went to the car.

"Chester, we are going to the Garden and Landscape Store this morning," Mother Williamson said. "Your grampy wants to take us out for lunch."

Once they arrived at the Garden and Landscape Store, Chester walked throughout the store, keeping his ears perked up. He didn't want to miss anything being said by the customers doing their shopping. Chester liked to visit the hamsters, gerbils, white mice, parakeets, and canaries at the landscaping store. He even liked watching the fish swim around in their aquariums.

Why, I see there is a new aquarium sitting against the wall. I think I will quietly walk over there and see what is in that aquarium. This is very interesting, a square box with gold items inside of it. The lid is opening and shutting. The rocks at the bottom sure are colorful. There are green plants sprouting up here and there, Chester thought to himself as he stared through the glass of the large aquarium. Suddenly, a large goldfish with huge bulging black eyes came swimming by. The large fish stopped in front of Chester and stared at him through the front glass of the aquarium. The only thing Chester knew what to do was tell this creature his name.

"Hi, my name is Chester. I must say you are very big in size, and your eyes do bulge outward," Chester remarked.

"I am a goldfish with very large eyes that bulge out extremely," the goldfish responded. "Not all goldfish look like me."

"What is your name? Where did you come from?" asked Chester.

"One question at a time, please," the goldfish said. "I don't have a name, and I came from my mama, who also is a goldfish."

"Where were you when you were with your mama?" Chester asked.

"My mama and I were a pet, and our owners had to move a long-distance away. They knew Mama and I wouldn't survive the long journey, so they placed us in this area where there was a large amount of water and fish. Mama really took good care of me, and we had fantastic adventures swimming together. Then the strangest thing happened. I became trapped in this large metal container."

"What made you want to swim inside a large metal container?" Chester asked, looking puzzled.

"I saw something wiggling around, and it glowed," the goldfish answered. "It looked very tasty. Once I swam inside, the wiggly glowing object disappeared, and a loud sound was heard. I turned around and saw the opening I had swam through was no longer there. I was trapped inside. Being trapped inside that metal container brought on discouragement and having no hope. I was tempted to give up. Mama stayed beside me, swimming around the large metal container. She reminded me that I had to have a strong will to survive and thrive. She told me that we were never promised an easy journey when swimming through the water of the large area our past owners placed us in. She encouraged me to keep going and never give up, even when our journey gets tough. She told me to restore my determination and endurance. This would provide the steadfast grit and tireless diligence needed to hold fast and swim against adversity toward restoration and victory. She advised me not to lose my drive to continue on my journey. Then the water started moving swiftly. That was when Mama told me she would see me again, and she hurriedly swam away. Mama must have known something was about to happen because soon after she left, two men came and took me out of the metal container and brought me here. I have been here since yesterday."

"That is very interesting. Would these two men happen to live in a stone cottage?" Chester asked.

"I don't actually know what a stone cottage is," the goldfish answered.

"No, you wouldn't know. Why would you know what a stone cottage is? You live in the water," Chester said.

"I have no idea what is going to happen to me next," the goldfish said. "Could you tell me about this place that I was brought to?"

"Sure! It is a garden and landscape store. My owners, Dave and Katy, own it. They are on a trip now, so my grampy and Scott are taking care of the store. People come and buy things for their garden and flower patches. Sometimes, children want a pet to bring home. That is where you come in at. Someone is going to want to take you home as their pet," Chester said.

"Why don't you take me home as your pet?" the goldfish asked.

"You would make a great friend. I have a cockatoo as a friend. He is standing over there on his wooden perch, watching the hamsters go around and round and round. His name is Samson. If I had you as my friend, I would name you Bubbles. You would really like Dave and Katy. When Grammy and Grampy come over, they bring me presents. It is a wonderful life!" Chester said.

"Take me home, Chester. Please take me home with you!" the goldfish said as he swam back and forth speedily in his large aquarium.

"I will see what I can do. It sure would be nice to have someone else to talk to at home. I know Samson would like you. If anyone can be persuaded to take you home today, that would be Grampy," Chester said.

"I am counting on you, Chester," the goldfish said.

"Don't worry, Bubbles, I have a plan. I just know it will work!" Chester exclaimed with great excitement.

"Chester, do you think I will see my mama again?" the goldfish asked.

"Your mama told you she would see you again before she swam away. What I need to do is figure out a way to find your mama in Cedar River. When I do that, I can tell her where you are," Chester said.

"Wouldn't it be fantastic if Mama could be with me at your home, Chester," the goldfish said in a delightful burble sound.

"Yes, that is what I was thinking," Chester answered.

"Chester, what is Cedar River?" the goldfish asked.

"That is the name of the water you and your mama were placed in by your first owners. I will talk to you soon. I first must go to my grampy and carry out my plan so you can live at my house. After you are brought to my house, where you will be safe, I will start thinking of a plan to find your mama. I have a lot of friends in Dark Woods who will be willing to help," Chester said.

"Chester, what is Dark Woods?" the goldfish asked.

"That is the area with tall trees, bushes, and flowers surrounding the Cedar River where you and your mama had fantastic adventures swimming together. I will soon be back. Watch and listen. My grampy will do anything for me!" Chester exclaimed.

Chester walked to the room where Father Williamson was arranging clay pots on a shelf. Chester did his twirl and meowed loudly. He then put his right paw up and looked toward the room where the goldfish was.

"What is it, Chester? What are you trying to say?" Father Williamson asked.

"Chester has done this before," Scott said. "Samson fell off his perch and passed out on the floor. Chester came to where Dave, Katy, and I were doing inventory. He did that fancy twirl and meowed very loud to get our attention. I think he wants us to follow him."

Scott, Mother, and Father Williamson followed Chester to the room where Bubbles was swimming wildly in his aquarium. Chester jumped up on the table, placed his paws at the top of the aquarium, and pressed his nose against the front glass of the aquarium. Bubbles came swimming up and stared at Chester.

"I think Chester likes that fish," Father Williamson said.

Chester gave out a loud *meow* and started licking the front glass of the aquarium.

"Chester, you can't eat the fish," Mother Williamson said.

"He's not trying to eat that goldfish. He is trying to tell us he likes that goldfish," Father Williamson said. Chester's head dropped, and he jumped to the floor. He curled up in a ball and started to whine loudly.

"What is wrong with Chester?" Scott asked.

"I don't know," Father Williamson said with a worried look on his face. "I hope he isn't sick."

Scott picked Chester up and held him close in his arms. "What is wrong, buddy?" Scott asked. Chester leaped from Scott's arms and jumped on the table again. He pressed his nose close to the aquarium glass and made his chirpy meow. Bubbles wasn't scared. He just floated in the water, staring at Chester.

"Is that all you got!" Bubbles exclaimed, swimming speedily around the aquarium. "Come on, really let them know you want me as your pet!"

"I think Chester and that fish have become true friends," Father Williamson said. "I am going to get things together and set up a large aquarium at Dave and Katy's home."

"Don't you think you should wait till Dave and Katy come home?" Mother Williamson said.

"No, that fish is coming home with Chester today," Father Williamson said sternly. "Believe me, Dave and Katy will be glad I did this."

"We have a larger aquarium in the back room."

"Scott, could you help me with this? I want to be sure I do this right."

"Sure, I can come to the house after we lock up today," Scott said. "I do know it takes a few days for the water to be right before we place fish in a new aquarium. What we will do is take the aquarium the goldfish is in now home. We will pour the water from this aquarium into a clean, large bucket and cover it with a lid. Then the goldfish can be placed in its original aquarium using the same water."

"What room would you like the aquarium to sit in?" Mother Williamson asked.

"The aquarium the goldfish is in would fit nicely in the sitting room," Father Williamson said. "When Dave and Katy return home, they can decide where to place the larger aquarium."

"That is a great idea," Scott said. "Dave is a pro at setting up a new aquarium."

Chester and Bubbles understood everything that had been said. Chester put his face against the aquarium glass again, and Bubbles swam up to Chester and gave him a big kiss.

"I'm glad I didn't feel that," Chester said.

"It's just my way of saying thank you, Chester," Bubbles said. "You are a true friend. I am looking forward to our visits together every day."

"I am looking forward to our visits too," Chester said.

"Anybody hungry?" Mother Williamson said.

"Yes, let's lock up and go to Sammy's Sugar Shack for lunch." Chester had a big surprise waiting for him at Sammy's Sugar Shack. Mother Williamson had called Sammy's Sugar Shack in the morning to let Sammy know they would be coming for lunch. Sammy had boiled some chicken for chicken sandwiches. She took some of the chicken and cut it up into small cubes and brought it to Chester for his lunch.

What a treat this is, and I soon will have another new friend to talk to at home. I am so excited to have Bubbles come and live with Samson and me. Maybe he can tell me more about what is going on at that stone cottage along Cedar River, Chester thought. Everyone else ordered cheeseburgers, curly fries, and malts.

That evening, Scott filled the aquarium that Bubbles was swimming in at the store with the same water that was in it. He used the same rock and the same artificial plants inside. He turned the light on at the top of the aquarium and also turned the power filter on. A small container of goldfish food was on a shelf under the table the aquarium was sitting on. "There, that should do it," Scott said. "I better be on my way. Peggy is waiting for me at her apartment in Springville. We are having pork chops and applesauce."

"Thank you for your assistance," Father Williamson said. "See you tomorrow at the store."

"Sure thing," Scott said as he walked out the door.

Chapter 25

Wednesday at Oklahoma City, Oklahoma

"Our third day together," Kevin said. "Everyone is present. It has been brought to my attention that some of you are concerned about your caseworker receiving the letters of recommendation before the end of this Friday. No concerns there. Tracy has received calls from all the people you contacted. The letters of recommendation will be looked at and placed with your application once they arrive. If there are any complications we foresee as Tracy and your caseworker read them, we will get in touch with you immediately. Any questions?" Kevin asked. "Okay, let's begin our next session, preservice training.

"During your preservice training, you will be doing the following: prepare yourself for foster care or adopting a child, create a basis for teamwork between yourself and your agency, form mutual supportive relationships with other parents and child welfare staff who will be able to help you throughout your journey, find answers to lingering questions you might have about whether you are ready to foster or adopt and what type of child you can successfully parent.

"There is also a home study process. After your training this Friday, you will be contacted by your caseworker to set up a date and time for your home study as long as your application has been accepted.

"A home study report includes family background, financial statements, and references, education and employment, relationships and social life, daily life routines, parenting experiences, details about your home and neighborhood, readiness and reasons about your wanting to adopt, references and background checks, and approval and recommendation of children your family can best present.

"The home study process could take between three to six months to complete. If you have a spouse or partner, both joint and individual interviews will be done. This also includes children living with you or those who live outside of your home. If you feel that you and the members of your household are not ready for a home study, you can ask to delay this step. The cost of an adoption home study can be anywhere between one thousand and three thousand dollars. Keep records and receipts because some of your out-of-pocket costs may be reimbursable if the services result in finalized adoption of a child from foster care.

"To speed up the home study process, have all necessary information supplied completely and accurately and don't delay filling out paperwork, scheduling medical appointments, or gathering the required documents. Tracy has typed the list for each of you. Before meeting with your caseworker today, please pick up your list at the front table. Tomorrow, we will touch on receiving a placement. Any questions?" Kevin asked. "Okay, see you tomorrow!"

"There sure is a lot to becoming a foster care and adoptive parent," Katy said as Dave drove the car into Mother and Father Williamson's garage.

"Yes, there is," Dave answered. "I am thankful we have a caseworker that helps us every step of the way."

"I am thankful too," Katy said.

Chapter 26

Wednesday at Sweetwater, Oklahoma

Father Williamson and Samson had already left for work at the Garden and Landscape Store. Bubbles was swimming happily in his aquarium. Chester was finishing his breakfast in the kitchen.

"Today is Library Day, Chester," Mother Williamson said. "Take your morning nap so you will be bright and bushy-tailed when we read a story to the children and help them with their craft." Chester walked to the sitting room and started to play with his catnip toys.

I sure do miss Dave and Katy. I love my grammy and grampy, but it just isn't the same without Dave and Katy here too. I do hope they come home soon, Chester thought to himself. *Maybe tomorrow, I will get a visit from Foxy Gent. Hoot Owl told Foxy Gent to check in with me in case I have any news on what is happening at that stone cottage along Cedar River. One can only hope*, Chester thought.

The morning went speeding by. Chester enjoyed a bowl of tuna and gravy for his lunch. Mother Williamson groomed Chester, making him look very handsome. Chester ran to the sitting room.

"Bubbles, when I get home from the library, I want to talk to you," Chester said.

"Okay, Chester, I will be looking forward to our chat," Bubbles said as he swam behind the tall foliage in his aquarium to take a nap.

"Chester, ride!" Mother Williamson shouted. Chester ran to his grammy with his collar in his mouth. Mother Williamson fastened the collar around Chester's neck, grabbed the black leash, and locked the door. The time spent at the library was fun and exciting, as always. Mother Williamson read the story *Spring Will Soon Be Here.*

Every child was given a packet of flower seeds from Dave's Garden and Landscape Store. The story that Mother Williamson read told what needed to be done to plant seeds in the ground so beautiful flowers and vegetables would grow in a garden.

The craft the children made was a kite. As the children flew their kites around the library, Chester would try to catch the tail of the kites.

"Come on, Chester, catch mine," Sally said.

"Look at mine, Chester!" Tommy shouted.

"You can't catch mine, Chester!" Billy boasted as he ran past Chester. Chester jumped on top of a bookshelf. He leaped from the bookshelf, spread all four of his legs outward, and grabbed the kite with his front paws. The children gasped when they saw Chester fly through the air.

"Look! Look!" the children shouted together. "Chester can fly!"

Down came Chester with the kite in his mouth.

"Chester, you did get my kite," Billy said. "And you can fly! You are amazing! I am glad you come to the library."

"Refreshments are ready," Miss Lilly said. All the children ran to the table and helped themselves to cherry wink cookies and cherry punch.

I am so tired after catching that kite. I am skipping the cookie crumbs that Sally shares with me. I am taking a nap, Chester thought as he jumped in the rocking chair and fell asleep.

After the children left, Mother Williamson helped Miss Lilly clean up the refreshments from the table.

"I wonder where Chester has gone off to?" Mother Williamson asked.

"I didn't see him while the children were enjoying their refreshments," Miss Lilly said. Mother Williamson and Miss Lilly walked to the reading area and saw Chester curled up in the rocking chair, sleeping soundly. Chester was having another dream. This dream was about his new friend, Bubbles, the goldfish.

Chester slowly opened one eye when he heard Mother Williamson's soft voice, saying, "Chester, wake up. It is time to go home."

Chester yawned and stretched. Mother Williamson rubbed him on his back and tummy. She then snapped his black leash on his collar, and they walked to their car. After arriving home, Chester immediately ran to the music room to finish his nap. After waking from his nap, he walked to the kitchen to eat his supper.

Mmmm! Beef and gravy! Grammy sure does know how to keep a kitty happy, Chester thought. After he finished his supper, he walked to the sitting room where Samson was standing on his perch and Bubbles was swimming in his aquarium.

"Why, Chester, you finally woke up," Mother Williamson said. "I think your new friend has been waiting for you."

Chester walked up to the aquarium and jumped on the table and stared at Bubbles as he enjoyed swimming back and forth.

"What can you tell me about what is going on in the stone cottage across Cedar River?" Chester asked.

"Why the interest, Chester?" Bubbles asked.

"Look, Bubbles, no one has used that stone cottage for a very long time. All the animals of Dark Woods are concerned for their safety. They saw lights flickering from the inside and smoke coming from the chimney," Chester answered impatiently.

"Well, it is like this, Chester, your friends in Dark Woods should be concerned," Bubbles said. "There are two trappers involved. Do you know what a trapper is?" Bubbles asked.

"No, I don't know what a trapper is," Chester answered.

"A trapper sets this device that looks like a cage in an area with food inside of it," Bubbles said. "Sometimes, the trap is placed in tall grass, and sometimes, the trap is placed in the river. The trappers wait patiently for an animal or fish to go inside the trap. That is when the door to the cage closes, and the animal or fish are unable to escape. The trappers come and check the cages and decide if they want to keep what they have caught and try to sell it or let it go free. I was trapped in a cage that was placed in the river. It was a large cage that had this wiggly thing moving. I swam toward the wiggly thing and grabbed it. After I grabbed the wiggly thing, I heard this loud sound. I turned around and saw the opening I swam through was no longer an opening. I had no way of leaving. I ended up at the place where you found me. I think these trappers sold me for a lot of money."

"That is terrible! I must go to Dark Woods tomorrow and warn all the animals of the danger they could be in. The animals are so happy where they live. The fish and other beings within Cedar River are happy too. I just want you to know, Bubbles, you were sold to a great guy. His name is Dave, and you don't have to worry about being sold again. You and I met, became true friends, and now you live in the same house as I do," Chester said wholeheartedly.

"Thank you, Chester," Bubbles said. "If it hadn't been for you, who knows where I would be and how I would have been cared for."

"Tomorrow, I need to make a run through Dark Woods to alert everyone what is going on in that stone cottage," Chester said seriously.

"I will be thinking of you, Chester, and waiting for your return," Bubbles said.

Chester walked up the spiral stairway to sleep in Mother and Father Williamson's bedroom. He knew it would be quiet, and he wanted to get up when Mother Williamson got up in the morning.

Chapter 27

Thursday at Oklahoma City

"You are on your way to completing our meetings this week," Kevin said. "I see all twenty-six couples are present. That is fantastic! Today, we will be talking about receiving an adoptive placement. This happens after the process of being matched with a child. The length of time between being notified that you have been selected as the adoptive family for a child or sibling group and receiving the physical placement of them in your home is dependent on many factors. Just as you will need time to prepare both physically and emotionally for the placement, so, too, does the child with the help of their caseworker, foster family, and others.

"The topics listed are, first, preparing children for placement. We have found that summer vacation, holiday breaks, or at the end of a school semester help the transition to go more smoothly. Second, scheduling preplacement visits with children. This can take place in your home, the child's foster home, or a neutral location. Be as flexible as possible. Ask your caseworker if the costs such as travel, meals, and overnight accommodations would be covered or reimbursed. Third, identifying post-placement resources. As adoptive parents, you may be eligible for other public benefits, such as a federal or state tax credit. Some employers offer benefits to employees who adopt. These can include paid or unpaid new parent leaves and financial assistance to help pay for adoptive costs. Fourth, preparing for the transition. Have a space prepared and move-in ready where your adopted child will sleep. This gives the child a warm welcome. You also may be able to find out the child's favorite colors and use these colors when decorating their room. You will also need to speak to your caseworker if it is wise to keep the child's current physician, dentist, and other medical and treatment providers or move to a provider with whom you and your family have established relationships. Another thing to do is make plans for school and extracurricular activities. Remember, all relationships, even the relationship between a parent and child, take time to take root. It has been found that during the first pre-placement visit, have some photos of you and the child together. This communicates the importance of the occasion. These pictures make great additions to the child's life storybook and family's photo story-book. And lastly, welcoming your child home. Homecoming day has arrived. There is no one-right-way approach to this event. It is a very important day that you will want to commemorate in future years. The time you have spent during visits getting to know more about the child you are adopting provides excellent clues to what will be meaningful and positive homecoming experiences for them. There is also the honeymoon period. The first weeks or months are commonly called this. Your caseworker will talk with you in more detail on this. There is also the post-placement supervision period. This is where the child's caseworker is required to see and talk with you and your child at least one time every thirty days. It is very important that you make time in your schedule for the caseworker visits. This is when you may discuss any issues that have arisen and ask questions that you may have.

"I will let you meet with your caseworker at this time. They will be giving you tips on how to help the child form attachments and build strong relationships among family members. Tomorrow is Friday, which will be our last day to meet. I will be presenting the topic 'finalizing an adoption.' You will then be meeting with your caseworker to set up a date for the home study. After that is completed, we will gather in this room, and a brunch will be enjoyed by all. You may visit with each other and say your goodbyes during that time. Any questions?" Kevin asked. "Okay, see you tomorrow!"

Chapter 28

Thursday at Sweetwater, Oklahoma

Chester woke up with a startle at two o'clock in the morning. He heard a sound that was quite familiar to him.

"Ack! Ack! Ack! Wooo! Wooo!" Chester jumped on the window sill and saw Foxy Gent. "Hey, Chester, I didn't mean to alarm you, but we need to talk," Foxy Gent said with a worried look on his face.

"What is it that can't wait till it is light outside? You know I can't get out of the house unless someone opens the front door or the back door," Chester answered sarcastically.

"Chester, do you remember the third story in your house?" Foxy Gent asked.

"Yes, I remember," Chester said.

"The window in the third story is open, and there is no screen," Foxy Gent said. "You could fly down."

"Well, that may be so, Foxy Gent, but there is one thing standing in the way," Chester said.

"What would that be?" Foxy Gent asked.

"The secret bookcase opening is probably not open. That is the only way up to the third story," Chester said.

"Would you be kind enough to go see if the secret bookcase is opened?" Foxy Gent asked.

What a cat doesn't have to do at all hours when it is still dark outside, Chester thought to himself as he scurried down the spiral stairway and walked down the hall into the music room. Chester was very surprised to see the secret bookcase entrance was not completely closed. Chester quietly walked through the opening. He didn't want to wake Samson up. He jumped on the banister post and slid the top to the right.

I need to push this lever so the bookcase will completely close. I do not want Samson, my buddy, to go through that bookcase opening and venture to the third-story room and fly out the open window. I might never see Samson again! Chester thought. After the bookcase closed completely, Chester ran up the oak stairway and jumped through the window. Putting all four of his legs outward, he flew through the air and landed on the ground safely. Foxy Gent was waiting patiently at the tall oak tree.

"Jump on, Chester," Foxy Gent said excitedly. "I want to show you something." As they crossed through a meadow within Dark Woods, there sat a large rectangular metal container with food in it. "Do you have any idea what this is for?" Foxy Gent asked.

"*Yes, I do. This is a trap. Bubbles, my goldfish friend, told me all about these traps. Bubbles was caught in one that was placed in Cedar River and sold to Dave, my owner, at his Garden and Landscape Store not too long ago. I was hoping you would show up like Hoot Owl told you to do, so I could tell you. Is this the only one you have found?"* Chester asked with a discouraged look on his face.

"Why, are there more?" Foxy Gent asked.

"*I don't know for sure, Foxy Gent. Bubbles said there were traps set all over the place in Dark Woods and along Cedar River,"* Chester answered.

"I wonder, perhaps we could get the door to close without going inside this trap." Foxy Gent suggested.

"*The door closes if someone goes in to eat the food. Animals and fish are captured and sold. I don't think it is legal. Bubbles told me that these two trappers at the stone cottage were the ones setting these traps. When they caught Bubbles, they brought him inside the stone cottage and put him in a large metal container of water. He didn't think he was going to survive,"* Chester said. "*What could we use to trigger that cage door to shut so no one would be captured tonight?"* Chester asked.

"Wait here, I have an idea," Foxy Gent said as he dashed to an old oak tree and grabbed a thick limb that had fallen to the ground. He placed the thick limb in front of the cage opening. "Okay, Chester, here is the plan," Foxy Gent said excitedly. "If anything will close that door to that trap, this will."

"*Question! Question!*" Chester screamed loudly.

"What is it now?" Foxy Gent asked in a very disgusted voice.

"*Who is going to put this piece of wood inside?*" Chester asked nervously.

"You are!" Foxy Gent said, pushing the piece of wood toward Chester.

"*Oh no! That is not going to happen! No! No! No! Do you think I was born yesterday? I mean, really! I could get caught in there, and those trappers will sell me!*" Chester snapped.

"You are right," Foxy Gent said. "That was a bad idea. I wouldn't want that to happen. We need you to help us in Dark Woods. You are the best thing that ever happened to all of us who live in Dark Woods."

"*Do you have a plan B??*" Chester asked.

"Yes, I will scoot the piece of wood in as fast as I can by pushing it with my back feet," Foxy Gent said. Foxy Gent took a run for the cage, did a half circle in the air, landed on his feet, and pushed the piece of wood with his back feet holding his tail up in the air.

Snap! The door on the front of the cage closed.

"There, mission accomplished!" Foxy Gent exclaimed, feeling very proud of himself. "Chester, come rest at my fox den. In the morning, we will alert all the animals to gather at Hoot Owl's tree house and announce the danger of what those trappers are doing throughout Dark Woods."

The following day… As the sun was starting to rise, Chester and Foxy Gent were gathering everyone to meet at Hoot Owl's tree house. Hoot Owl walked out, giving a big yawn and asked, "Whooo called a meeting?"

"Chester and I did," Foxy Gent answered. "There is danger among Dark Woods to all who live within it. Large, dangerous cages are sitting in the tall grass, along flowery meadows and in Cedar River. You must stay away from the cages. If you enter a cage, you will be captured, and you won't be able to escape. You will never have the freedom you now have or see your friends in Dark Woods again."

"When the men who set those traps find that piece of wood inside one of their traps, those trappers will know we are on to them and their illegal dirty tricks," Chester said.

Everyone agreed not to go close to the cage. They also promised to alert others who lived in Dark Woods and were unable to be at the meeting that morning.

"Foxy Gent, would you know how to get to that stone cottage?" Chester asked.

"Yes, there is a pathway that leads to a bridge we can walk over to get to the other side of Cedar River," Foxy Gent answered.

"Let's go there. I want to investigate that stone cottage," Chester excitedly said.

"Jump on my back," Foxy Gent said. Chester jumped on Foxy Gent's back, and off they went like a streak of lightning through Dark Woods. As they got closer to the stone cottage, Chester jumped off Foxy Gent's back.

"Stay close by, Foxy Gent. I might have to make a run for it," Chester said.

"Okay, I will be a few feet away, waiting and watching," Foxy Gent answered.

Chester walked slowly up to the door of the stone cottage and reached for the black handle. He began pushing the handle up and down. The door opened slowly.

"Chester, do be careful," Foxy Gent said.

"I just want to look inside. That is what detectives do, and I am the detective of Dark Woods," Chester said. Chester pushed the door open, and there standing inside were two tall men looking down at him.

"Who do we have here, Mac?" Roni said.

"A very nice-looking cat," Mac answered. "He would bring a nice amount of money at a pet store. Look at that M on his forehead. That is the mark that a Maine coon cat has."

"He has tufted hairs coming out of his ears too," Roni said. Chester started hissing and growling at the two men. "Get him!" Roni shouted. Mac grabbed Chester's tail so he couldn't get away. Chester turned and bit Roni on the hand as he tried to lift Chester up from the ground.

"*Foxy Gent, help! Help!*" Chester meowed frantically. Foxy Gent ran speedily toward Mac and took a large bite out of his arm.

"Oh, I have been bitten by a fox!" Mac shouted as he let go of Chester's tail.

"Come on, Chester, jump on my back," Foxy Gent said. "We need to get out of here!"

Roni ran inside the stone cottage and got his shotgun. "I'll get you for biting me, cat!" Roni shouted in an angry voice.

"Get that fox too!" Mac exclaimed. "I am really injured here! The blood is gushing out of my arm."

Chester jumped on Foxy Gent's back, and off they went, taking cover within the tall oak trees so they could no longer be seen.

"Are you okay, Chester?" Foxy Gent asked as he ran up the front porch steps of Chester's home. "You look really stressed."

"*That was too close for comfort. I didn't know if I was going to be able to get away from that Mac and Roni. They were tall and really strong!*" Chester said.

"What made you want to go inside that stone cottage?" Foxy Gent asked.

"*I wanted to see if any animals had been caught. Bubbles told me those men bring their catch to a building and then try to sell them the following day,*" Chester answered.

"Chester, I would be careful and think things out before doing something like this again," Foxy Gent said. "You know the saying 'Curiosity will kill the cat.' You were curious today. I don't want anything to happen to you."

"*That's why I wanted you there with me. I knew you could help me if I needed it. Thanks, Foxy Gent,*" Chester said, giving him a friendly wink.

"Always obliged to help a good buddy," Foxy Gent said, giving a wink back.

"Keep me posted, friend. I will always be there for you and everyone in Dark Woods," Chester remarked in a friendly manner.

"I will do that," Foxy Gent answered. "Do you think I could meet that true friend of yours, Chester, you call Bubbles sometime?" Foxy Gent asked.

"Sure thing, Foxy Gent. I will work on a plan to sneak you into the house. Bubbles would like to meet you," Chester said.

"Later, Chester," Foxy Gent said as he ran toward Dark Woods.

"Yes, later, Foxy Gent. Say hi to Foxy Lady," Chester said.

"Will do, good buddy!" Foxy Gent shouted as he disappeared into Dark Woods.

Mother and Father Williamson had awakened and were coming down the spiral stairway to see who was ringing the bell on the front porch.

"Chester, where have you been?" Mother Williamson said as she opened the door. "You must be starving! Come to the kitchen, and I will open a can of egg and cheese bits with white sauce for you." Chester slowly walked to the kitchen and collapsed on the tile floor beside his food dish and water bowl.

I am so tired. I can barely lift my head to eat. I must eat and drink before I sleep. I don't want to get sick. I might be needed in Dark Woods again, Chester thought. Chester slowly lifted his head up and took a bite of his food. Then he took another bite and another bite. It wasn't long before Chester had eaten all his food. *I must have been a hungry kitty*, Chester thought as he drank some water and strolled slowly to the sitting room to take a nap.

Samson was screeching. "Samson out! Samson out!"

"I am coming, Samson," Father Williamson said as he walked into the music room and unhooked the latch to Samson's cage. "What's the matter? Didn't your mysterious visitor let you out this morning?" Father Williamson asked. Samson ignored Father Williamson and started down the hall toward the kitchen, making his clickety-clack, clickety-clack sound with his feet as he walked on the hardwood floor.

"Chester, Chester, did you find or hear anything in Dark Woods?" Bubbles asked.

"Yes, Bubbles, but I need to sleep right now. I am totally exhausted. We will talk when I wake up," Chester said.

"Okay, good buddy," Bubbles said. "I understand. Would you like me to sing you a song?" Bubbles asked.

"No, Bubbles. Thank you for the gesture, but I really need peace and quiet. Perhaps another time," Chester answered as he curled up, closed his eyes, and was asleep in a few seconds.

At one o'clock in the afternoon, Chester woke up.

"Chester, you are awake," Bubbles cried out.

"Hi, Bubbles, what's new?" Chester asked.

"Not much, Chester," Bubbles answered. "Can you tell me anything about Dark Woods?" Bubbles asked.

"Sure can! Foxy Gent and I found the cage, tripped the door on the front of the cage so it would close, and alerted as many as we could about staying away from the cage. Foxy Gent and I are really concerned there might be more cages throughout Dark Woods," Chester said.

"If there are other traps set, they wouldn't be far from the stone cottage," Bubbles said. "The two men in that stone cottage don't have enough energy to walk very far other than that meadow across Cedar River."

"Well, that is good to know. How do they get the cage across Cedar River to the stone cottage when they capture something?" Chester asked.

"They have a motorboat," Bubbles answered. "They check their traps morning, noon, and evening before dark."

"Thanks, Bubbles, for all the information," Chester said.

"Anytime, good friend," Bubbles answered.

Chester walked to the kitchen and saw a bowl of chicken and gravy in front of his white cupboard in the kitchen. He gobbled it up, stretched, and noticed the door was open to the enclosed back porch. Chester walked in and jumped on a window sill and saw Mother Williamson pounding these small poles on the ground. She then had string and was tying the string to the poles.

"What is my grammy doing?" Chester asked himself.

Chester scooted outside the screen door of the enclosed porch. He wanted to investigate those poles and strings Mother Williamson was working on.

This is very strange to have in the yard, Chester thought. Mother Williamson was in the white shed, putting the string and hammer away. Chester walked into the white shed and jumped on the workbench.

"Hello, Chester," Mother Williamson said. "What do you think of my garden?" Mother Williamson asked.

That is a garden. It isn't like the gardens Dave has at his Garden and Landscape Store, Chester thought.

"We are going to grow a lot of vegetables," Mother Williamson said. "Not something you like to eat, but we sure enjoy them. I am counting on you, Chester, to keep those bunnies away." Chester just swayed his tail back and forth as Mother Williamson talked.

"I wonder what a bunny is?" Chester asked himself.

"Come along, Chester. I am closing the shed door," Mother Williamson said. Chester jumped down off the workbench and ran out of the white shed. He walked to the area that was to be a garden. He saw a long brown thing scooting its way slowly on top of the dirt.

Is this a bunny? What is so harmful about this? I bet Bubbles would know, Chester thought as he picked up the crawly creature in his mouth, placed it on the back porch step, and tapped at the screen door.

"Come on in, Chester," Mother Williamson said as she opened the screen door to let Chester inside. Chester ran in with the crawly creature in his mouth. He could barely hang on to it. It was so wiggly and slippery. Chester ran through the kitchen, down the hall into the sitting room, jumped on the table where the aquarium was, and gently put the crawly creature down.

"Bubbles, come here. I need to ask you something," Chester said. Bubbles awakened and swam to the front of the aquarium.

"Hey, Chester, what's up, good buddy?" Bubbles asked.

"Could you tell me what this creature is?" Chester asked, holding the squirmy creature in his mouth.

"Get it away from me!" Bubbles shouted. "That is how I got caught in that metal container of Cedar River and sold! I thought it looked tasty, and when I entered the cage, that wiggly thing got away.

I was unable to escape like that wiggly thing did. I was taken by those two men who live in that stone cottage in Dark Woods."

"Tell me, Bubbles. What is it? Is it a bunny?" Chester asked, looking very confused.

"No, it is a worm," Bubbles answered. "They do no harm except to a fish like me. If you don't know about them, a fish can get caught, sold, or eaten."

"I had no idea, Bubbles. I did not mean to upset you. I will bring it back outside. I am so sorry. It has been a stressful day for me also," Chester said.

"Yes, take it outside. Please take it outside!" Bubbles exclaimed.

"I am taking it outside now," Chester said as he put the earthworm in his mouth and walked to the kitchen. He made his chirpy meow sound and did a twirl.

"Boy, I am getting a little dizzy here," said the earthworm. "Please let me go free."

"What do we have here?" Mother Williamson asked as she looked down and saw the earthworm in Chester's mouth. "Chester, some of your friends cannot come into the house. Come, Chester, take your friend outside." Mother Williamson opened the back porch screen door so Chester could go outside with the earthworm. Chester placed the earthworm in the garden area.

"What is your name?" Chester asked.

"Eddy," the earthworm answered.

"What are you?" Chester asked.

"I am an earthworm," Eddy answered.

"Oh, I thought you were a bunny," Chester said.

"Next time you don't know what something is, ask," Eddy answered. "You can also go to a library and read a book that tells and shows you what a bunny is. That was very upsetting to me. That large thing swimming in the water could have eaten me."

"I am sorry. I won't let it happen again," Chester said as he put his head down on his front paws and gave a sigh. After Eddy, the earthworm, was out of sight, Chester walked up the steps and tapped on the screen door.

"Come in, Chester," Mother Williamson said. "Your supper is ready. Samson has already eaten and is waiting for you in the sitting room to keep him company. I am sure Bubbles will be happy to see you too."

Chapter 29

Friday at Oklahoma City

"Welcome back!" Kevin said. "This has to be an exciting day for all of you! Our topic today is finalizing an adoption. After a child is placed with your family, the court with jurisdiction over the child retains that jurisdiction until the adoption is legalized. A caseworker will visit you and your child at least once each thirty days between placement and legalization. The purpose of these visits is to see how things are going. Adoptions are legally binding agreements. It is very rare for adoption to be challenged in court by a child's birth relative. More than ninety-eight percent of adoptions from foster care remain legally intact after the final step in the journey to adoption. It is very important that you have the Foster Care and Adoption Agency guidelines for our state of Oklahoma. At each table is another copy of these guidelines to take with you. These guidelines are very important to have, so you can refer back to them if necessary. I will now let you meet with your caseworker so you can schedule a time for the home study process."

"Hi, Dave and Katy," Evelyn, the caseworker, said. "Welcome back to my office. I would like to set up a time to do a home study at your home in Sweetwater, Oklahoma. I have next Wednesday available at ten o'clock in the morning."

"That would be fine," Katy said.

"Will both of you be able to be present?" the caseworker asked.

"We can be," Dave said.

"It would be better if both of you are present when my team and I come," Evelyn, the caseworker, said.

"We will both be there," Katy said.

"Well, all right then, ten o'clock next Wednesday morning," Evelyn, the caseworker, said as she handed an appointment card to Katy. "I am trying to get as many done as I can before Easter. We will be that much closer to getting the adoption process completed. If there are any improvements that need to be made, you have plenty of time to do so. If a cancellation needs to be made, please let me know, and I will reschedule. Oh, I also wanted to let you know your three letters of recommendation have been received. They have been placed in your file for future reference. That is all I have for you today. Enjoy the brunch and visiting with everyone, and have a safe drive home."

"Thank you for all you have done and for stepping Dave and me through this entire process," Katy said.

"We are looking forward to the home study next Wednesday," Dave said.

*****

"The brunch sure was delicious," Katy said.

"Yes, I have never seen that much food on display," Dave said.

"It was good to get all the other couples' phone numbers and addresses," Katy said. "I am looking forward to keeping in touch by sending letters to them, a Christmas card each year, and calling them every now and then."

"You know what would be fun," Dave said.

"No, what?" Katy asked.

"Having a get-together in the summer once a year," Dave said.

"That is a fantastic idea," Katy said. "Let's get through this home study process first."

"Yes, I definitely agree with that," Dave said. "Will be nice to get that out of the way."

"It sure will be good to see Samson and Chester," Katy said.

"It will be nice to sleep in our own bed," Dave said.

Dave and Katy arrived home at three o'clock in the afternoon.

"We are home!" Katy shouted. Chester came running when he heard Katy's voice. Katy immediately picked him up and ran her fingers through his long thick orange hair.

I am so glad you are home. I missed you so much. I love Grammy and Grampy, but I love you and Dave too. Please don't be away this long again. This is the second time you have been gone this long. The first time was after that day I had that satin pillow with your wedding rings attached to it around my neck. I had to alert help from Dark Woods to come and help Grammy and Grampy when those intruders broke into your house. Thank goodness things were much quieter during this time you were gone, thought Chester as he purred loudly.

"Welcome home, Dave and Katy," Mother Williamson said, giving them both a hug. "I hope you had a good time."

"We had a marvelous time," Katy said.

"Your father and Samson will be here shortly," Mother Williamson said. "I made a chicken casserole, lettuce salad, home-made rolls for supper, and an apple pie for dessert that we can enjoy. You go ahead and unpack your luggage while I set the table."

"We are home," Father Williamson said as he took Samson from his shoulder and placed him on the floor.

"Samson, how are you?" Dave asked.

"Did you miss us?" Katy asked.

"Samson, cracker! Samson, cracker!"

"Samson, you know it is time for your supper," Katy said. "You may have a cracker after you eat your supper. I hope Grammy and Grampy haven't spoiled you by giving you a cracker every time you ask for one."

"Oh, no, we kept a strict list of what time Samson and Chester ate and what they ate," Mother Williamson said. "Let's sit down and eat before it gets cold."

"I am so glad everything went well while we were gone," Katy said as she took her last bite of a homemade roll.

"Your father and I were relieved that everything went well too," Mother Williamson said.

"Everything went great at the Garden and Landscape Store too," Father Williamson said. "People sure are anxious for Easter and spring to get here. A lot of Easter lilies have been ordered, and packets of garden and flower seeds have been purchased."

"That is good to hear," Dave said. "I am looking forward to returning to work on Monday."

"We will probably leave tomorrow morning around nine o'clock," Mother Williamson said.

"How did it go with Chester and Samson at night?" Dave asked.

"Now that you brought it up, we do have a question," Mother Williamson said. "Have you solved the mystery of how Samson gets out of his cage?" Mother Williamson asked.

"It is still a mystery," Dave said. "We have not been able to solve it."

"We wake up in the morning, and Chester is in the sitting room, watching cartoons on television, and Samson is standing on his wooden perch munching on a cracker," Mother Williamson said.

"Yes, the cracker box is open on the counter," Father Williamson said.

"If we get the mystery solved, you will be the first to know," Katy said, giggling.

"There was one morning Samson was still in his cage," Mother Williamson said. "It was Thursday, wasn't it, John?" Mother Williamson asked.

"Yes, Chester slept in our bedroom that night," Father Williamson said. "After we awakened in the morning and were walking down the spiral stairway, the bell on the front porch was ringing. I opened the door, and there standing on the porch was Chester."

"We have no idea how Chester got outside!" Mother Williamson exclaimed. "We made sure all the doors were locked and the windows were shut except the window in our bedroom. There was no way Chester could have gotten out of that window because there is a screen covering it."

"It has happened before, Mother and Father," Katy said.

"We have no idea how Chester gets outside during the night," Dave said. "But we do know he is unable to get back in the house on his own."

"Who rang the bell on the front porch?" Katy asked.

"That is another mystery that needs to be solved," Mother Williamson answered.

"If anyone can solve any of these mysteries, it will be Detective Katy," Dave said, chuckling. "You better get to it, Detective!" Dave exclaimed. Everyone laughed.

"John, are you going to tell Dave and Katy who the new member is in their home?" Mother Williamson asked.

"Follow me," Father Williamson said, walking to the sitting room.

"You brought the large goldfish home!" Dave exclaimed.

"Yes, Chester fell in love with it, and I couldn't say no," Father Williamson answered. "I have no idea what his name is."

"Bubbles! Bubbles!" Samson squawked.

"There you go, Dad. We now know the goldfish's name is Bubbles," Dave said.

"There is a new aquarium ready to be set up on the back porch," Mother Williamson said.

"We thought it would be best if you set it up, Dave. We didn't want to do something wrong and hurt the goldfish," Father Williamson said.

"No problem," Dave said. "I will be happy to do it."

"You both sleep in tomorrow morning," Mother Williamson said. "It has to be nice to sleep in your own bed after being gone for five days. I will make sure Samson and Chester are fed and have a great breakfast prepared for the both of you."

"Thank you, Mother and Father, for all you do," Katy said.

"Thank you," Dave said.

Chapter 30

Mother and Father Williamson left at nine o'clock Saturday morning after a scrumptious breakfast consisting of ham and cheese omelets, hash browns, buttered toast and choice of strawberry jelly or orange marmalade, hot coffee, and fresh-squeezed orange juice.

"I sure am glad everything went well while we were gone," Katy said.

"Chester and Samson seem to be happy too," Dave said. "Chester slept all night at the foot of our bed, and Samson stood on top of the dresser mirror."

"I sure would like to solve that mystery of how Samson gets out of his cage and the door is still latched," Katy said, giving a slight giggle.

"Like I said before, some mysteries are never solved," Dave answered. "No harm is done except for the cracker crumbs on the kitchen floor. What can I help you with, Katy?" Dave asked.

"We should go through the house and make sure everything is clean and in place before the home study this Wednesday," Katy said.

"What about the enclosed porch?" Dave asked.

"Yes, that definitely needs a thorough cleaning," Katy answered. "I haven't touched that since last fall," Katy said. "If we have time, we need to check the yard for any fallen limbs and sticks on the ground. I want the property to look very inviting inside and outside."

"Would you like me to place the two rocking chairs, table, and swing on the front porch?" Dave asked.

"Yes, that would be great," Katy said. "Don't forget to remove the wreaths from the front doors. The lights on the gazebo and the artificial tree in the gazebo need to come down also."

"Let's leave the lights on the gazebo," Dave suggested. "I think it would look really pretty when we invite the couples we met at the Foster Care and Adoption Agency over for a barbeque," Dave said.

"I never gave that a thought," Katy said. "I agree. It would look nice to have the gazebo lit up on a summer night."

"Okay, I will get right to it," said Dave.

"I will be out to help as soon as I finish up in the kitchen," Katy said.

"I can't believe it is already five o'clock in the afternoon," Katy said.

"Yes, time sure goes fast when you are having fun," Dave said.

Dave and Katy both laughed as they walked into the house.

"The enclosed porch looks great!" Dave said.

"Thank you. It is nice to have it open again," Katy said.

"This will be the first time for Samson to enjoy it. I better bring another wooden perch home so Samson has a place to sit on the enclosed porch and enjoy the view with the rest of us," Dave said.

"We need to get the blue cat condo from the other side of the bookcase by the oak stairway," Katy said.

"I will go get it right now," Dave said. "Katy, come here!" Dave shouted.

"What is it?" Katy asked, walking through the bookcase opening.

"I feel a draft coming from the third-story room," Dave said.

"We better go check it out," Katy said.

"Empty as usual, but the window is open," Dave remarked with a puzzled look on his face.

"Perhaps, Mother and Father had come up and decided to air out the room and forgot to close the window," Katy said.

"No harm done," Dave said. "I will close the window. Would you like to help me set up that other aquarium on the back porch?" Dave asked.

"Sure, I always wanted to learn the correct way to set up an aquarium so the fish won't die," Katy answered.

"First, we have to make sure the aquarium is placed out of direct sunlight," Dave said.

"That shouldn't be a problem with the wicker shades I purchased," Katy said. "I will make sure the wicker shades are always pulled down on these two windows of the enclosed porch when the sunlight is shining in."

"We now need to make sure there is a five-inch space between the aquarium and the wall to accommodate the filter."

"The table the aquarium is sitting on seems to be level," Katy said.

"That is great. We don't want a tipsy table," Dave said. "Let's go to the kitchen and rinse the gravel and colored rock in clean water."

"I will start placing some of the clean gravel and rock in the bottom of the aquarium as you continue rinsing the remaining gravel and rock," Katy offered.

"It is very important to slope the gravel and colored rock up toward the back," Dave said. "A clean plate would work great to move the gravel and colored rock toward the back."

"I will go to the kitchen and get a plate," Katy said.

"You take the plate and start sloping the gravel and colored rock toward the back of the aquarium while I slowly pour water into the aquarium," Dave said. Since the water was from the kitchen faucet, Dave added the proper amount of chlorine neutralizer liquid so Bubbles, the goldfish, would not be threatened by chlorine or chloramines within the tap water. "Now it is time to assemble and hang the power filter on the back of the aquarium," Dave said. "Where do you think we should attach the thermometer so it will be easy to monitor it?" Dave asked.

"I think placing the thermometer right here would be easy for us to monitor it," Katy suggested.

"I agree. Good choice!" Dave exclaimed. "Now the heater needs to be assembled and installed underwater level near input to the filter," Dave said.

"I will go to the kitchen and rinse the artificial plants with clean water," Katy said.

Dave and Katy placed the artificial plants and large stones throughout the aquarium. Dave finished filling the aquarium with water. "Oh, I can't forget to fill the filter with water also," Dave said.

"Katy, you do the honors and plug the filter and heater in the outlet on the wall."

"I am so excited!" Katy exclaimed as she placed the plug in the wall outlet.

"Great, everything is working as planned," Dave said with a pleased look on his face. "I couldn't have done it without you, Katy. We have to wait twenty-four hours before placing Bubbles in the new aquarium. Katy, would you write me a note to remind me to bring home a bottle of 'live nitrifying bacteria' tomorrow?" Dave asked.

"Sure, what is live nitrifying bacteria for?" Katy asked.

"It quickly establishes biological filtration and cycle of the aquarium," Dave answered. "We will see how it goes once we place Bubbles in the water. After four weeks, we can add other fish to the aquarium also so Bubbles won't be lonely."

"What kind of fish would we be able to add to the aquarium?" Katy asked.

"Rainbow fish, angelfish, rasboras, barbs, danios, and kissing fish," Dave said.

"Let's give it some thought," Katy said. "Bubbles seemed to be quite content by himself in his aquarium in the sitting room. I will write down goldfish food on the note too."

"Yes, we can't forget to feed Bubbles," Dave said, giving a chuckle.

"I am worn out!" Dave exclaimed.

"Me too. It is already six o'clock in the evening," Katy said as she collapsed in a wingback recliner in the sitting room. "I just thought of something," Katy said.

"What is that?" Dave asked.

"Do we show the third story of the house during the home study?" Katy asked.

"I don't think that is necessary," Dave said. "I don't want everyone to know about that bookshelf opening to another area of the house, including that stairway under the oak stairway that leads to a tunnel ending at the concrete pavilion."

"I just hope it doesn't hurt our chances of adopting if they find out from someone other than us," Katy said. "Kevin said to be honest in everything."

"Let's think about it," Dave said. "I am too tired to make a decision at this time."

"Are you hungry?" Katy asked.

"After that large breakfast, I don't need anything to eat," Dave said. "Let's just sit here and watch television and relax."

"It sure is good to be home," Katy said.

"Yes, it sure is," Dave said.

Dave and Katy fell asleep in their wingback recliner chairs. Chester was curled up in his cat bed, and Samson flew to the top of the cat condo to sleep.

Chapter 31

"Well, Katy, it's Monday, the day for our home study," Dave said.

"I am so nervous," Katy said. "What are we going to say if they ask how many stories our home has?" Katy asked.

"We will tell them the truth," Dave said. "Three stories and a basement. Remember what our caseworker told us. Being honest is the key through the entire foster care and adoption process."

"You are right," Katy said. "Honesty goes a long way and proves what kind of person you are. I am going to bake these two loaves of bread, and there is homemade vegetable soup simmering on the stove. I learned the smell of baked bread and homemade soup simmering puts the finishing touch when showing a home."

"Where did you hear that?" Dave asked.

"My grandma Dove told me," Katy said, laughing softly as she walked to the kitchen.

"I would have liked to meet your grandma Dove," Dave said. "She sounds like a very sweet lady."

"She was, Dave," Katy answered. "When things settle down, I will tell you all about my grandma Dove."

"I am looking forward to it," Dave said, giving her a kiss on the cheek.

At ten o'clock sharp, the bell on the front porch rang.

"Hello, welcome to our home," Dave said with Katy standing beside him.

"Come in! Come in!" Katy said anxiously.

"Good morning, Dave and Katy," Evelyn, the caseworker, said. "I would like to introduce my team members, James and Don."

"Very nice to meet you," Dave said, shaking their hands.

"As you take us through your home, we will be asking questions," Evelyn said. "You start the tour, and we will follow."

"You certainly have a beautiful home," Evelyn said. "Everything is well kept and up to date. This is a two-story home with a basement, am I correct?" Evelyn asked.

"It is a three-story home with a basement," Dave said. "The third story is used for storage, and it is the same length and width as the entire house."

"Oh, I see," Evelyn said. "Like a large attic."

"Yes," Dave said. "You could call it that."

"We don't have to tour that area," Evelyn said. "Something smells good!"

"Would you and your team like to stay for lunch?" Katy asked. "Homemade bread and vegetable soup!"

"Thank you, but we need to be on our way," Evelyn said. "I want to check out the Sugar Creek Lutheran Church, Twin Cedar Bridges Park, and the business places in Sweetwater. It is listed that you and Katy are owners of the Garden and Landscape Store located on Jefferson Street."

"Yes," Dave answered. "It is in both of our names since Katy and I are married."

"The team and I will be stopping there too," Evelyn said.

"I will see you there," Dave said.

"Is there a restaurant in Sweetwater where we could eat lunch?" Evelyn asked.

"Sammy's Sugar Shack," Katy said. "You will love it! Fabulous service and delicious food."

"Great!" Evelyn exclaimed. "Thank you for showing us your home. I will be in touch with you soon."

"Thank you for coming and enjoy the rest of your day," Katy said.

"Now we wait," Dave said. "I need to go to work. I will let you know how it goes when Evelyn and her team come to the Garden and Landscape Store."

"What about Scott?" Katy asked. "We can't let anyone know about this."

"No worries. I am giving Scott the afternoon off," Dave said.

"That was great thinking," Katy said as she gave Dave a big hug. "See you when you get home."

Later, Dave walked into the Garden and Landscape Store.

"Scott, you can go now," Dave said. "Have a great afternoon off."

"Thanks, Dave. See you tomorrow," Scott said as he walked out the door.

Dave was busy helping a customer when Evelyn and her team, James and Don, walked into the store.

"I just want to browse," Evelyn said. "If I need anything, I will let you know." Evelyn walked to the front, where Dave was standing behind the counter. "You have a very nice store, Dave. I am impressed with the entire town of Sweetwater."

"Katy and I sure like it here," Dave said. "There is never a dull moment."

"I noticed a cockatoo in the other room," Evelyn said. "He wants a cracker."

"That's Samson," Dave said with a smile. "He is always wanting a cracker. We keep him on a very strict diet."

"I also was impressed with your Maine coon cat back at the house," Evelyn said. "He is so well behaved. Slept all the while you and Katy showed us your home."

"Chester is like any other cat," Dave said. "He sleeps, eats, plays, sleeps, eats, plays." Evelyn, James, and Don laughed.

"Thank you for letting us see your store," Evelyn said. "We must be on our way. It is a three-hour drive to Oklahoma City."

"Thank you for coming," Dave said. "If you are ever in Sweetwater again, be sure to stop in."

"We will do that," Evelyn said.

Dave locked the door to the Garden and Landscape Store and drove home with Samson standing on the top of the passenger seat, looking out the window.

"We are home!" Dave shouted.

"Supper is ready," Katy said.

"It went good at the store when Evelyn and her team stopped by," Dave said. "Samson tried to get Evelyn to give him a cracker."

"Samson, did you try to trick Evelyn into giving you a cracker?" Katy said as she placed a bowl of bird seed in front of the white cupboard for him to eat.

"She was really impressed with the entire town of Sweetwater, the Twin Cedar Bridges Park, and Sugar Creek Lutheran Church," Dave said.

"I am glad," Katy said. "I can't wait to hear from her," Katy said.

"I am anxious to hear from her too," Dave said.

Chapter 32

Katy was busy in the kitchen, making a cherry pie and apple pie. "There, I will wrap these pies with plastic film, cover them with aluminum foil, and place them in the freezer," Katy said to herself. "They will be ready to bake on Saturday, the day before Easter Sunday." The phone rang. Katy hurriedly brushed the flour from her hands and ran to the sitting room.

"The Middletons, this is Katy," Katy said, completely out of breath.

"Hello, Katy! This is Evelyn, your caseworker. Am I calling at a bad time? You sound out of breath."

"No! No! I was rolling out a pie crust," Katy said. "My parents are coming for Easter."

"How nice!" Evelyn said. "I think it is wonderful when families can get together during the holidays. The reason for my call is I have great news to share with you and Dave. Since Oklahoma City is a three-hour drive, I was wondering if you and Dave could meet me at a restaurant in Springville, Oklahoma, this evening. That would reduce your drive to one hour."

"Yes, we will work it out!" Katy said excitedly. "Let me call Dave, and I will call you back immediately."

"Great!" Evelyn exclaimed. "I will be waiting for your call."

Katy immediately dialed the phone number for the Garden and Landscape Store.

"Garden and Landscaping, this is Dave. How may I help you?" Dave asked.

"Dave, it is Katy. I just got a call from our caseworker, Evelyn. She has exciting news to share with us. She would like to meet with us at a restaurant in Springville to reduce our drive to one hour. I am supposed to call her back. Dave, can we go? Please! Please! Say yes, we can go!"

"Of course, we can go," Dave said. "I get off at five o'clock. It won't take me long to shower and get dressed."

"What about Chester and Samson?" Katy asked.

"Make arrangements with the receptionist at the veterinarian clinic in Springville so we can drop Chester and Samson off before going to the restaurant," Dave said.

"Okay, I will call you back after I get everything arranged," Katy said. "Love you!"

"I love you too," Dave said.

Katy called her caseworker, Evelyn, first.

"Hi, Evelyn. Dave and I will be able to meet you at Springville," Katy said.

"Great!" Evelyn exclaimed. "I will see you both at the Somerset Restaurant around half-past seven this evening."

"We will be there," Katy said.

Katy then dialed the veterinarian clinic in Springville.

"Springville Veterinarian's Clinic, this is Tammy. How may I help you?"

"Hi, Tammy, this is Katy Middleton. I was wanting to drop my Maine coon cat, Chester, and cockatoo, Samson, at your pet facility for a few hours while Dave and I go out for supper."

"What time will you be here?" asked Tammy.

"Approximately half-past six," Katy answered.

"That should work out fine," Tammy said. "We will be waiting for your arrival."

"Thank you," Katy said.

Katy dialed the Garden and Landscape Store again. Before Dave could say anything, Katy immediately began talking.

"Hi, Dave, everything is arranged," Katy said.

"Okay, honey, I will be home shortly after five o'clock," Dave said.

"I will have your clothes laid out," Katy said.

"Thanks, sweetie. We should be on the road by quarter to six," Dave said. "Have Chester and Samson fed and ready to go."

"I will. Love you," Katy said anxiously.

"Love you too. See you soon," Dave said.

Dave was so excited. He took his shower, got dressed, and everyone was in the car heading for Springville, Oklahoma, at half-past five. After stopping at the Springville Veterinarian's Clinic to place Chester and Samson at the pet facility, Dave and Katy walked into the Somerset Restaurant. Dave gave their names to the hostess, and she escorted them to a booth.

"Hello, glad you made it," Evelyn said. "Order anything, my treat."

"Would you care for something to drink?" the waiter asked.

"I will have water with a slice of lemon on the side," Dave said.

"I will have the same," Katy said.

After the waiter placed the beverages on the table, he asked, "Are you ready to order?"

"I will have the baked chicken, mashed potatoes with gravy, and mixed vegetables," Katy said.

"I would like the homestyle chicken, mashed potatoes with gravy, and green beans," Evelyn said.

"And you, sir, what can I get you?" the waiter asked.

"I would like the grilled pork chops, mashed potatoes with gravy, and green beans," Dave said.

"A loaf of homemade bread with butter and lettuce salads with several choices of dressings will be delivered to your table for you to enjoy while you wait for your meal to arrive," the waiter said.

"While they are preparing our food, I want to let you know why we are meeting at such short notice," Evelyn said. "Twins were found in a car wreckage two weeks ago. They are now six weeks old. The parents did not survive the accident. The agency does not want to split the children up. If we can't find anyone who has gone through the five-day training to adopt the twins, we will have to put them up for adoption individually. So my question is, would you consider adopting the twins?" Evelyn asked.

"Are they boys or girls?" Dave asked.

"One boy and one girl," Evelyn said. "They are in very good health. We did go through the waiting process to see if there were any relatives who wanted to take the twins. No one has come forward, and the waiting period is up."

"Do you have pictures?" Katy asked.

"Yes, I most certainly do," Evelyn said as she laid the picture of the twins in front of them.

"Oh, Dave, look at them. They are beautiful," Katy said, trying to hold back tears of happiness.

"May we see them and hold them?" Dave asked.

"I can arrange that you see them," Evelyn said. "I need your answer tonight if you are willing to adopt both of them. I will leave you alone to talk in private. I need to go to the powder room."

"Oh, Dave, twins," Katy said. "I never thought anything like this would happen to us."

"I'm all for it, Katy," Dave said. "We have plenty of room in our home to raise twins, and I am sure Mother and Father Williamson will help us get the nursery ready and care for them."

"I agree," Katy said. "We can talk to them when they come for Easter tomorrow."

"Have you made a decision?" Evelyn asked.

"Yes, we want to adopt the twins," Dave said.

"What do we need to do?" Katy asked.

"Both of you sign right here and date it," Evelyn said as she pointed to the lines on the document. "I will sign under your names. It will probably take two to three weeks to get all the paperwork done. That will give you time to prepare your home for your children."

"Where are the twins staying now?" Katy asked.

"They are at the Methodist Hospital here in Springville," Evelyn said. "Would you like to see them tonight?"

"Yes!" Dave and Katy answered together.

"After we eat our meal, we will go," Evelyn said. "I will call the hospital to let them know we are coming."

Later, at the Methodist Hospital in Springville Oklahoma, Dave and Katy could hardly hold their excitement back as they followed Evelyn through the hospital entrance doors.

"Dave, would you push floor three," Evelyn said as the elevator doors closed.

Dave, Katy, and Evelyn walked down the hall and stopped in front of a large glass window. Evelyn tapped on the door and spoke to a nurse quietly. A curtain opened from the large glass window, and there stood two nurses holding a baby in their arms.

"Oh, Dave, look at them. They are beautiful," Katy said. "I want to hold them and rock them and sing to them."

"What is the waiting period?" Dave asked.

"I am sure everything will go through speedily," Evelyn said. "Your home passed with excellent marks for the home study. You both are definitely at the top of being wonderful parents to adopt after looking at the marks given during your training session at the Foster Care and Adoption Agency. The children are safe in the hospital and won't be moved until they are in your arms and brought to your beautiful home. You need to prepare your home for the twin's arrival immediately. When everything is approved, you will be contacted to come and pick up the twins. You will need to have car seats for each of them before taking them home."

"Dave, we need to go home and get things ready for our son and daughter," Katy said. "Mother and Father are coming tomorrow for Easter. I can't wait to tell them. I know they will stay and help get the house ready."

"Have you thought about names?" Evelyn asked.

"We can choose names for them," Dave said, raising his eyebrows.

"Yes, you may give them new names if you like," Evelyn said.

"Can we think about it over the weekend?" Katy asked.

"Take your time. I will put your last name, Middleton, on their name tags of their nursery basket right away," Evelyn said.

"Thank you, Evelyn," Katy said.

"Thank you for all you have done," Dave said.

"Let's go home," Katy said.

"Let me know what you decide for their first names so I can finish the paperwork," Evelyn said. "I also want to let you know since you are adopting both children who are siblings, there is no adoption fee to pay, and there won't be any cost for your home study when my team and I came to look at your property."

"Thank you, Evelyn. We will call you when we have made a decision on the children's names," Katy said.

"Yes, thank you, Evelyn," Dave said.

Dave drove to the veterinarian clinic to pick up Chester and Samson.

"Samson, home! Samson, home!" squawked Samson as he perched himself on the edge of the seat behind Dave.

"Katy, I don't want you to worry about anything," Dave said. "I will help you any way I can after the children come to our home and while they are growing up. I will always be there for all of you. I will be a good husband and father."

"Thank you, Dave. I love you, and I know you will be a good father," Katy said. "I already know because you are a good husband. I wonder what Chester is going to think?" Katy asked.

"He will love it, especially when they get old enough and they can give him a lot of attention," Dave said.

"I hope he doesn't show jealousy," Katy said.

"He never got jealous when I entered your life," Dave said.

"That is true," Katy said.

"We just have to remember Chester is part of our family too," Dave said. "He will probably be a good protector of our children. Samson will be fine with it too. I am sure. He will have more people to talk with and sneak a cracker to him." Katy and Dave laughed.

Chapter 33

"Today is Library Day, Chester," Katy said as she placed a bowl of egg and cheese bits with white sauce in front of the white cupboard in the kitchen. Chester gave a loud meow and did a twirl when he heard it was Library Day. "You seem eager for Library Day!" Katy exclaimed.

I am anxious to read up on what a bunny is. There is no place like a library. Eddy, the earthworm, told me to read about bunnies in a book at the library, Chester thought to himself as he finished his breakfast.

"Chester, ride!" Katy shouted. Chester came running with his collar in his mouth. Katy placed the collar around Chester's neck and grabbed the black leash from the hook, locked the door, and walked to the SUV. All the children had arrived at the library and were waiting in the reading room to have a story read to them. Sally was sitting in the wingback rocking chair, waiting for Chester to jump on her lap.

"Come on, Chester, it is my turn to hold you while the story is being read by Katy," Sally said with joy in her voice. Chester jumped up and curled himself comfortably on Sally's lap. Katy held a large book up for all the children to see.

"Today, friends, I am going to read a story about a bunny," Katy said.

Bunny! Bunny! Chester thought as he jumped from Sally's lap and sat upright in front of Katy so he could see the front of the book. *Come on! Come on! Begin reading the story. I want to learn about bunnies,* Chester thought as he gave a chirpy meow and started twirling around in a circle.

"Looks like Chester is excited to hear the story too," Katy said. As Katy read the story, Chester listened intently, giving all his earnest and eager attention.

I sure have my work cut out for me keeping bunnies out of Grammy's garden, Chester thought as Katy closed the book. *I want to stay here and look through this book again*, Chester thought. The children enjoyed refreshments, which consisted of cutout egg-shaped cookies with different frosting colors on each one. Lemonade was served as the drink. Their craft was a picture of a bunny sitting in a flower garden that the children could color at home.

Later, as Katy drove in the driveway, she noticed that Father and Mother Williamson's car was parked at the front of the house. "Look, Chester, Grammy and Grampy have arrived," Katy said. "They are going to spend Easter Sunday with us."

Mother and Father Williamson met Katy and Chester at the front door.

"We decided to come early," Mother Williamson said. "I wanted to plant some vegetable seeds and flower seeds in the garden that I started in the back of your house. I hope that is okay."

"That is fine," Katy answered. "You are welcome any time, and you may stay as long as you wish."

Chester and Samson were busy eating their supper while Dave, Katy, Mother, and Father Williamson enjoyed the steaks that Dave grilled. They had a baked potato, green beans, hot homemade rolls, and a lettuce salad with Italian dressing.

"You chose a good time to come," Dave said. "This is the night we place Bubbles, our goldfish, in his new aquarium on the enclosed porch. Katy, I brought home another treasure chest to place in the aquarium. Would you place it in the aquarium and hook it up to the pump so the lid will open and shut?" Dave asked.

"Sure!" Katy exclaimed.

"While Katy is doing that, your father and I will clean up the supper dishes," Mother Williamson said.

"We will have our dessert on the enclosed porch and watch Bubbles explore his new aquarium," Katy said.

Dave carefully placed Bubbles in a large plastic bag with water from his aquarium that was in the sitting room. As Dave carefully carried the plastic bag to the enclosed porch, Chester and Samson were following right behind him. Dave opened the plastic bag and placed it in the water of the aquarium that was placed in the enclosed back porch. Bubbles instantly swam out of the plastic bag. Chester jumped on the table in front of the aquarium, and Samson flew up to the table beside Chester.

"Hi, Chester and Samson," Bubbles said as he swam swiftly through the water. "I love my new home. It is larger than the other one I was in."

"Yes, it is larger. A fish your size needs a large place to swim in. You will love the enclosed porch. There is so much to see in the backyard. I will sleep right here so you won't get scared. Believe me, before the night is over, Samson will probably be standing somewhere close too," Chester said.

"You are a true friend, Chester," Bubbles said. "Thank you for wanting to stay with me during my first night. Please thank Samson for me too."

"You can thank him yourself, Bubbles. After Dave and Katy are asleep, Samson will be wanting out of his cage. I know how to open the cage door to let Samson out. I always make sure I latch the door after closing it so Dave and Katy won't have any idea how Samson gets out of his locked cage. I even know how to get Samson a cracker from the cracker box in the kitchen cupboard," Chester said.

"You are a true friend, Chester," Bubbles remarked.

Chapter 34

The following morning, Chester opened his eyes and saw that Bubbles was doing fine in his new aquarium. Samson was standing on his perch and was fluffing his feathers outward and back in place.

"Come on, Samson, let's go have our breakfast," Chester said.

"Well, looks like our mysterious visitor was here again last night," Katy said. "I see Samson slept in the enclosed porch with you, Chester." Chester and Samson ignored Katy and walked to their bowl of food and started eating.

"Today, Chester, I am going to plant vegetable seeds and flower seeds in the garden," Mother Williamson said cheerfully. "Would you like to help?" Mother Williamson asked. Chester followed Mother Williamson outside and enjoyed the cool breeze and soft grass while she planted the seeds. Within three hours, the planting was done. "There, the seeds have been planted," Mother Williamson said as she brushed dirt from her garden gloves. "With a nice rain, those seeds will sprout and begin to grow tall." Chester just swayed his tail back and forth without a care in the world.

"Katy, what can I help you with?" Mother Williamson asked as she walked into the kitchen.

"I just put a chuck roast in the oven," Katy answered. "Would you like to peel some potatoes?" Katy asked.

"Sure, I will be happy to do that," Mother Williamson said. She peeled, washed, and quartered the potatoes, and she placed them beside the chuck roast. "How about some carrots?" Mother Williamson asked.

"Yes, that would be great," Katy answered.

Mother Williamson peeled the long carrots, cut the ends off, and placed those alongside the chuck roast also. "That should be done when Dave and my sweet hubby come home from the Garden and Landscape Store," Mother Williamson said as she closed the oven door.

"Let's go sit on the enclosed porch and keep Bubbles company," Katy said. "I will bring some hot tea and pecan sandie cookies in for us to enjoy."

"That sounds yummy," Mother Williamson said.

Bubbles seemed to be enjoying his new aquarium. He swam back and forth, looking through the glass. Katy pulled the wicker shades up that had blocked the direct sunlight from Bubble's aquarium. She then opened one of the windows. Bubbles was amazed when he could hear the birds singing.

"We're home!" Dave exclaimed as he lifted Samson from his shoulder. "Is supper ready?" Dave asked.

"Yes, we are eating on the back porch," Katy said.

"Let's eat," Father Williamson said.

"While we eat, Dave and I have something we want to tell you," Katy said. Father Williamson gave grace.

"What do you and Dave want to tell us?" Mother Williamson asked as she passed the meat platter of sliced roast, quartered potatoes, and carrots to Father Williamson. Dave and Katy smiled at each other as Katy slid the picture of the twins toward her parents. "Who is this?" Mother Williamson asked.

"We are adopting twins," Katy said. "Dave and I have talked about it, went through the Foster Care and Adoption Agency training, and we found out last night from our caseworker, Evelyn, that this baby boy and the baby girl survived a car accident a few weeks ago. Their parents did not survive. The agency wanted the children to stay together when they are adopted."

"Katy and I signed papers, and we got to see them at the Methodist Hospital in Springville," Dave said.

"They are so beautiful!" Mother Williamson exclaimed.

"What are their names?" Father Williamson asked.

"Right now, the names on their nursery basket are Baby Boy Middleton and Baby Girl Middleton," Katy said. "You are the first to know about this."

"We sure could use some help making the music room into a nursery," Dave said. "We have approximately two weeks to get everything ready before our children come home."

"Dave and I haven't had much time to discuss names," Katy said. "I thought we would do that after Easter sunrise services and the breakfast potluck at Sugar Creek Lutheran Church."

"You are still planning to go with us, aren't you?" Dave asked.

"Yes, we are looking forward to it," Mother Williamson said. "My goodness, John, we are going to be grandparents."

"We will help you with anything," Father Williamson said.

"My goodness, Dave, this is identical to what happened to you as a child, but you were never adopted," Mother Williamson said.

"Yes, Mother, my miracle never happened," Dave said. "I am so happy to become the father of these two children. I plan to tell them when they are older that they made our miracle come true, and we made their miracle come true."

"That is so sweet," Mother Williamson said.

Chapter 35

The grandfather clock in the sitting room struck five o'clock in the morning. Everyone was getting ready to leave for the Easter sunrise service at the Sugar Creek Lutheran Church. Chester and Samson were finishing their breakfast as Dave walked into the kitchen.

"When do you want to let your parents know that we have decided on names for our son and daughter?" Dave asked.

"I think now would be a good time," Katy said. They walked into the music room where Mother and Father Williamson were conversing on how the music room could become a nursery.

"Mother, Father, Dave and I have agreed on names for our children," Katy said.

"Tell us!" Mother Williamson said.

"We have decided on the name for our son to be Kyle James Middleton, and the name for our daughter will be Kylie Sue Middleton," Katy said.

"I like those names," Father Williamson said.

"They are beautiful names," Mother Williamson said. "What are your thoughts on letting people know about adopting Kyle and Kylie at the sunrise services today?" Mother Williamson asked.

"We never thought about that," Katy said. "What are your thoughts, Dave?" she asked.

"The best way to let everyone know at one time would have Pastor Mike announce it before the breakfast potluck," Dave suggested. "What do you think, Katy?" he asked.

"I think that would be a very good idea," Katy said. "Should I call him before we leave?"

"Yes, Pastor Mike needs to know before the sunrise services start," Dave said.

Katy dialed the number on the phone in the sitting room. "Good morning on this beautiful Easter Sunday!" Pastor Mike said.

"Good morning to you, Pastor Mike," Katy said. "Dave and I have great news to share with you and would like you to announce it before the breakfast potluck today."

"What is this news you want me to share with our congregation?" Pastor Mike asked.

"Dave and I are adopting twins!" Katy exclaimed.

"That is absolutely wonderful, Katy!" Pastor Mike said joyously. "What a wonderful thing to share on Easter Sunday! Do these children have names?" Pastor Mike asked.

"Yes! Our son's name will be Kyle James Middleton, and our daughter's name will be Kylie Sue Middleton," Katy answered proudly.

"All right, I will be sure to announce this joyous news and let you and Dave converse with everyone during the breakfast potluck," Pastor Mike said. "See you soon at sunrise services."

"We are getting ready to leave now," Katy said.

It was a beautiful day for the sunrise service at Sugar Creek Lutheran Church. Everyone gathered under the open-shelter building and sang songs, said prayers of thanks, and read the story of Jesus Christ's resurrection. After the services, everyone gathered in the basement of the church and filled their plates with scrambled eggs, bacon, sausage, hash browns, pancakes and waffles with maple syrup, toast, English muffins, all flavors of jelly, orange juice, grape juice, coffee, and water. Pastor Mike gave the prayer before anyone began to eat. After the prayer, he made the announcement.

"I have something wonderful to share with all of you today," Pastor Mike said. "It is not only a wonderful day to celebrate our Lord's resurrection, but it is also a wonderful day for Dave and Katy Middleton. They have become parents of adopted twins through the Foster Care and Adoption Agency in Oklahoma City. The baby boy was named Kyle James, and the baby girl was named Kylie Sue. Be sure to congratulate Dave and Katy on becoming parents while you enjoy this delicious breakfast. Dave and Katy will be happy to share their experience in becoming adoptive parents of these two children with all of you today."

"Ahhh!" was the sound heard when the congregation heard the news of Katy and Dave becoming parents of adopted twins. Mother and Father Williamson had a wonderful time letting everyone know how excited they were becoming grandparents.

"Dave, how did you keep this quiet from me and everyone else in Sweetwater?" Scott asked.

"It wasn't easy, Scott, especially when I had to make a sudden change in our schedule to have you work that week when I wanted to be with Katy," Dave said.

"So that is what you and Katy had planned," Scott said.

"Yes, that was the week we attended the meetings at the Foster Care and Adoption Agency in Oklahoma City," Dave said. "Thanks again for filling in on such short notice."

"Anytime, boss, I might have to ask you to switch Saturdays or work a week without me in the future," Scott said. "Congratulations on becoming a father."

"Thank you, Scott," Dave said. "We will be getting together with Peggy and you soon."

"If you need any help getting things ready at your home for the arrival of your baby boy and baby girl, just let us know," Scott offered. "We are here to help in any way."

"I will remember that, and thanks again," Dave said.

"That was a busy Easter sunrise service," Mother Williamson said.

"The breakfast potluck sure filled me up," Father Williamson said.

"I thought it would be good if we wait till this evening and have hot ham sandwiches, potato salad, and baked beans for supper," Katy said.

"That would be fine with me," Dave said. "I want to do some measuring to see how we can turn that music room into a nursery."

"I will help you with that," Father Williamson said.

"Katy, you and Mother need to go to Bob's Discount Furniture Store tomorrow and look at nursery furniture," Dave said. "Your father and I will be going to the Garden and Landscape Store to work."

"You are going to stay?" Katy said.

"Yes, you are going to need help, Katy," Mother Williamson said.

"We have nothing to go home to," Father Williamson added.

"I am so happy!" Katy exclaimed.

Chapter 36

At ten o'clock Monday morning, Katy, Mother Williamson, and Chester walked into Bob's Discount Furniture Store to look at nursery furniture.

"Hi, Katy. What can I help you with today?" Bob asked.

"We are going to change the music room into a nursery," Katy said.

"Are you wanting white furniture or a type of stained wood?" Bob asked.

"What type of stained wood do you have on display?" Katy asked.

"I have oak, walnut, and cherry," Bob answered.

"I know I don't want white," Katy said. "The house has oak-wood throughout it. I think oak will be my choice."

"Follow me, and I will show you the room with oak nursery furniture," Bob said.

"Oh, look, Mother, I really like the chest of drawers and cribs," Katy remarked.

"Yes, what a clever idea to use the top of the chest of drawers as a changing table when the children need clean diapers and clothes on," Mother Williamson said.

"I like that idea too," Katy said.

"As you see, the chest of drawers is wider, longer, and not as tall as a usual chest of drawers for that reason," Bob said.

"This is the set I want," Katy said. "I will take two sets."

"Two sets?" Bob asked.

"Yes, Dave and I have adopted twins," Katy said with a smile.

"That is wonderful. Congratulations!" Bob exclaimed. "I will get this written up immediately. We have another set in the warehouse."

"Would you have four wingback upholstered rocker/recliners?" Katy asked.

"Yes, follow me," Bob said. "We have many colors to choose from."

"What do you think, Mother?" Katy asked.

"Choosing different colored rockers would give the nursery some color within it," Mother Williamson suggested. "I like the maroon upholstered rocker, and your father would like the olive-green upholstered rocker."

"Dave would like the navy-blue upholstered rocker, and I have my eye on that gold upholstered rocker," Katy said. "Do you have two oak tables that could sit in between the upholstered rockers?" Katy asked.

"I actually have two oak tables that match the chest of drawers you chose for the nursery," Bob said. "I also have a long oak table that you can set items on, and it, too, matches the chest of drawers."

"That would work for the small refrigerator and microwave," Mother Williamson said.

"I would be happy to show it to you," Bob said.

"I would like to see it," Katy answered. They walked to the room that had living room furniture displayed.

"Here is the table I was telling you about," Bob said.

"That would be perfect," Katy said. "We will take two of those also."

"You might want to consider laying carpet over the oakwood floors," Bob suggested.

"Laying carpet over the wood floor would be quieter when we walked on it," Katy said. "Do you have carpet that doesn't need to be stapled or glued to the wood floor?" Katy asked.

"Yes, when Dave has the floor measurements, tell him to leave twelve inches of the oakwood floor showing beside the walls," Bob said. "When you want to change the room back to a music room, you can roll the rug up and place it in another room or store it."

"Thank you. I like that idea," Katy said.

"Choose the color and pattern you like and have Dave call me on the measurements," Bob said. "I can have the items delivered next week."

It was going on six o'clock in the evening. Katy and Mother Williamson had placed a large bowl of spaghetti and meatballs and a tray of toasted garlic bread on the table of the enclosed porch.

"There's the goldfish!" Father Williamson exclaimed. "How is he doing in his new aquarium?" Father Williamson asked.

"He seems to be doing fine," Katy said. "Mother, Chester, and I were gone most of the day. We went to Bob's Discount Furniture Store and chose the furniture for the nursery. We can lay a carpet over the wood floor without gluing it or stapling it. In future years, when we make the room into a music room again, the rug can be rolled up and used in another room or stored."

"What a fantastic idea!" Dave exclaimed.

"When you measure, leave twelve inches of the wood floor showing beside the walls," Katy said. "I will call Bob when you have the measurements."

"Dad and I will measure it after we eat," Dave said.

"What is the name of that fish?" Father Williamson asked.

"I think Chester named him, and Samson let us know what the name was," Dave said as he placed another scoop of spaghetti on his plate.

"You know Samson, he can't keep anything quiet," Katy said, giggling.

"Well, are you going to tell us?" Father Williamson asked.

"Tell you what?" Dave asked, looking confused at Father Williamson.

"What is the name of the goldfish?" Father Williamson asked.

"Oh, Bubbles," Dave said, giving a chuckle.

"I like that name," Mother Williamson said. "Bubbles seems to enjoy his aquarium on the enclosed porch."

"He seems to enjoy listening to the birds sing and watch the tree limbs sway back and forth also," Katy said.

"Your father and I have an idea to present to both of you," Mother Williamson said. "We have been doing some serious thinking after you told us about Kyle and Kylie becoming your children, and we realize how busy you will be. Taking care of the twins and Dave having to go to the Garden and Landscape Store during the week will be a full schedule for both of you. Babies require a lot of care and attention."

"What your mother is trying to say is, we would like to sell our home in Oklahoma City and build a small cottage on your property so we are right here to help in any way," Father Williamson said.

"We will pay for the cottage plus the electricity and water bill and any other bills that would come up. We have nothing keeping us at our home in Oklahoma City," Mother Williamson said. "Yes, we have our friends and our church, but we can always go there to visit, and you are welcome to come along when we visit if you like."

"Talk it over between the two of you and let us know what you decide," Father Williamson said. "The sooner, the better, so we can get things underway of selling our house in Oklahoma City and begin building the cottage."

Dave and Katy looked at each other and smiled. "Dave and I were thinking the same thing," Katy said.

"Yes, we would like you to live on our property and help us with the children," Dave said.

"We have a lot to do," Katy said.

"Let's sit down and make a list of what needs to be done," Mother Williamson said.

"That room you want to make into a nursery comes first," Father Williamson said.

"Make a list of all the items you will need for the babies before their arrival, such as diapers, clothes, etc.," Mother Williamson said. "I spoke with Peggy, Scott's girlfriend, and she would like to give you a baby shower. The shower is for both Dave and you to attend."

"That sounds wonderful!" Katy said. "I will get a pad of paper and pen to start a list now while we enjoy our meal." As Katy was writing down the items needed for the nursery and their two children, Kyle and Kylie, Mother Williamson came walking into the enclosed porch with dessert.

"What do you think about my bunny cake?" Mother Williamson asked as she set the plate holding the cake in the center of the table.

Bunny! Bunny! thought Chester as he leaped toward the table and *splat*! He landed in the middle of the beautiful bunny cake. *I have to attack! Grammy told me to keep bunnies away!* Chester thought, realizing what a mess he had made. Dave, Katy, Mother, and Father Williamson all gasped when they saw Chester lying in the middle of the bunny cake. Chester had chocolate cake and icing all over him and the table.

"A bath is waiting for you, Chester," Dave said as he picked him up and carried him to the shower to spray him off.

I am in really big trouble! That is the only time I get a bath! Chester thought.

"I am sorry, Mother," Katy said in an apologizing voice. "The cake looked beautiful and scrumptious."

"I will be happy to make another one."

"I don't know what got into Chester to do this!"

"I don't know either," Mother Williamson said. "Something triggered Chester to attack my bunny cake!"

Katy, Mother, and Father Williamson had everything cleaned up when Dave walked into the kitchen with Chester in his arms.

"That was a surprise," Dave said, giving Mother Williamson a hug.

"Yes, it was shocking but yet amusing," Mother Williamson said.

"I wish I had my movie camera when Chester took his surprising leap into that cake," Katy said. Everyone laughed.

"I have no idea why Chester would do such a thing," Dave said.

"We might never know," Katy answered. "Another mystery for me, Detective Katy. We have to be careful not to say the word G-O-L-I-A-T-H around Samson and B-U-N-N-Y around Chester."

"Let's go for a drive," Father Williamson suggested.

"May Chester come?" Katy asked.

"Sure, Chester is always welcome," Mother Williamson answered.

"I thought we could take a drive to Twin Cedar Bridges Park," Father Williamson said. "We have received a lot of rain this spring. I would like to see how high the river is."

"That's a great idea," Dave said. They drove through the Twin Cedar Bridge and followed the road that led to Cedar River.

"The river is flowing quite rapidly," Father Williamson remarked.

"Yes, it definitely is," Mother Williamson replied.

"This is the time of year when the rapids cause water aeration of the river, which will give Cedar River a better water quality," Dave said.

"Look, Chester," Katy said. "Cedar River is really moving along today."

Perhaps this will stop those two men from crossing the river with their boat to check that trap. Maybe the fast-flowing water will make that cage float away, Chester thought as he watched closely while being held in Katy's arms. Dave took a large quilt out of the car and placed it over the grass so everyone could sit down. Father Williamson went to the car and opened the trunk and took out a picnic basket.

"Well, let's see what is in this picnic basket," Mother Williamson said. "Well, look at this, ham on buns, and you have your choice of mayonnaise or mustard to spread on your bun if you like. Potato chips and a thermos of iced tea. Sorry, no bunny cake."

Chester heard the word bunny. He jumped off the quilt and did a twirl and made a chirpy meow. Everyone's mouth dropped open with fear, wondering what Chester was about to do next. Katy grabbed Chester and held him in her arms and tried to calm him by talking softly to him. "It's all right, Chester. Calm down," Katy said. Chester started purring and went back to his spot on the quilt. "I am going to say something. Listen very carefully. Don't say a word until I am finished," Katy said. "I believe the word B-U-N-N-Y is upsetting Chester. Why, I do not know, but we cannot use that word around him any longer."

"Oh my, Chester was with me when I was making my garden, and I told him it was his responsibility to keep the—"

"Mother, stop!" Katy interrupted. "Don't say B-U-N-N-Y."

Mother Williamson's eyes got huge in fright. "Oh, yes, uh, B-U-N-N-Y out of the vegetable garden," Mother Williamson said.

"Well, now we know why Chester attacked that cake earlier today," Dave said. "We are going to have to work with him on this B-U-N-N-Y word."

"One mystery has been solved by our great Detective Katy," Father Williamson said. "Is everyone ready to go home?" Father Williamson asked.

"Yes, it has been quite a day," Mother Williamson said as she began to place things in the picnic basket.

Chapter 37

Two weeks had gone past. The music room was soon turned into a nursery. Everything was moved out of the room, except for the harp, Chester's cat bed, and Samson's wooden perch and cage. The books on the bookshelves were also stored away. Katy wanted to use the shelves to place toys and stuffed animals for their children to see and play with. Dave made a beautiful shelf to be hung in the room so Katy could display her violin. That way, she could play the violin anytime she wanted. The largest item that had to be moved was the baby grand piano. The legs had to be removed, and the piano had to be tipped on its side on a cart with wheels so it would roll through the open bookcase and be placed along the wall across from the hidden oak stairway.

Bob's Discount Furniture Store delivered all the nursery furniture and installed the carpet over the oakwood floor.

The furniture consisted of two oak chests of drawers, two oak baby cribs, four wingback rocking chairs that were upholstered, two small oak tables placed between the recliner-rocking chairs, and two long oak tables placed on each side of the walk-through fireplace. Father Williamson and Dave placed the small refrigerator on one of the oak tables and a microwave on the other oak table.

Peggy and Scott gave the baby shower at Dave and Katy's home. Everyone from Sweetwater was invited. It was a full house that afternoon. Some of the gifts were disposable diapers, baby clothes, blankets, bedding, musical mobiles that would be hung over each crib, diaper bags, car seats, stuffed animals, rattles, high chairs, musical swings, bouncy chairs, and walkers on wheels. Father and Mother Williamson rolled in two oak cradles that Father Williamson built at the Garden and Landscape Store.

"You can roll these in your bedroom now and then so the babies can be close to you and Dave while you sleep at night," Mother Williamson said.

"Thank you, everyone, for coming and for the wonderful gifts," Katy said.

"Thank you," Dave added.

"We have refreshments for everyone," Peggy said. "Come to the kitchen and help yourself."

Everyone enjoyed cupcakes with blue and pink frosting swirled on top, squares of vanilla ice cream with blue and pink rattles imprinted on top, blue and pink candies, nuts, crimp bread with cheese spread or ham salad spread. A delicious pink punch was served along with coffee and iced tea. After the last guest left, Dave, Katy, Mother, and Father Williamson helped Peggy and Scott clean the kitchen and put everything back in place.

They all retired to the sitting room to chat for a while.

"I think we are ready for our children to come home," Katy said.

"I believe you are right," Dave said.

"Katy, have you given any thought to what you plan to do about Wednesday afternoons at the library?" Mother Williamson asked.

"I need to call Miss Lilly and let her know I won't be able to come," Katy said.

"When you call, ask her if she would like me to fill in during your absence," Mother Williamson said.

"That would be fantastic, Mother," Katy said. "I will call her tomorrow. I need to call Evelyn, our caseworker, and let her know we have decided on names for our children," Katy said. "She might be able to tell us when we can bring Kyle James and Kylie Sue home."

"Why don't you give her a call now," Dave suggested. "She carries a mobile phone with her wherever she goes."

"I think I will," Katy said.

Katy began dialing the phone number while everyone sat quietly listening. Suddenly, the phone started to ring. Katy immediately stopped dialing and spoke on the phone receiver.

"The Middletons, this is Katy speaking."

"Hello, Katy. This is Evelyn, your caseworker. Have you and Dave chosen names for the children yet?" she asked.

"Hello, Evelyn. I was in the process of calling you," Katy said. "Yes, Dave and I have chosen names for our children. Baby boy Middleton's name will be Kyle James Middleton, and baby girl Middleton's name will be Kylie Sue Middleton."

"The names are beautiful," Evelyn said. "I will finish the paperwork with their names. Is everything ready at your home for Kyle and Kylie?" Evelyn asked.

"Yes, we had a very nice baby shower today and received many nice gifts," Katy said. "The nursery is set up where the music room once was."

"Do you have any assistance in caring for the children after you take them to their home?" Evelyn asked.

"Yes, my mother, Mary Williamson, and father, John Williamson, have offered to stay and help," Katy answered.

"That is fantastic," Evelyn said. "Have you purchased two car seats for the children?" Evelyn asked. "It is Oklahoma's law that children birth to two years of age must be placed in a rear-facing car seat while traveling in a vehicle."

"Yes, that was a gift we received today at the baby shower," Katy answered. "The car seats are very well padded, and the part the child sits in is easy to remove and can be carried around as an infant seat. It is a convertible car seat, which is able to change into a forward-facing and booster car seat in the future."

"That is great!" Evelyn said. "Someone did their homework when they purchased the car seats as a gift for your children."

"The car seats have been placed in the backseat of our SUV, and we are ready to take our children to their new home," Katy said excitedly.

"Would tomorrow work for the both of you?" Evelyn asked.

"Yes, Dave and I will make it work," Katy answered with enthusiasm.

"I will meet you at the Methodist Hospital in Springville at ten o'clock in the morning," Evelyn said. "I will be waiting at the front desk."

"Dave and I will see you then," Katy said.

"Our children come home tomorrow," Katy said as she placed the receiver on the phone.

"That is wonderful news," Mother Williamson said joyfully. "I was talking to your father about the Library Day on Wednesdays. He has offered his assistance also to fill in at the library so you won't be alone with the children for the time being."

"Thank you, Father. That is very kind of you," Katy said. "I know the children at the library will love hearing you read a story to them."

"I'll do anything for a cookie," Father Williamson said jokingly.

"We will make sure Chester goes along also," Mother Williamson said. "It would do him good to get away now and then too."

"I think that is a good idea," Dave said. "A change of scenery would be nice for Chester".

"We must be going," Peggy said as she got up from her chair.

"Thank you for the wonderful shower you and Scott planned for Dave and me," Katy said, giving her a hug.

"Yes, thank you for helping us clean up afterward too," Mother Williamson said.

"Scott and I want to give all of you time to know Kyle James and Kylie Sue and let them become familiar with their new surroundings before we come to visit," Peggy said.

"Thank you," Katy said.

"If you need anything, be sure to call," Scott said, shaking Dave's hand.

"Thank you, Scott," Dave said. "Take care and have a safe drive home."

"We need to talk about the cottage you want to be built," Dave said. "This is a great time to start building."

"Where do you plan to build it?" Father Williamson asked.

"Let's take a walk outside, and I will show you," Dave said.

They walked outside toward the tall oak trees leading to Dark Woods. "I don't think it is wise to build close to the tall oak trees," Dave said. "Katy, what do you think about building the cottage in the area across the front driveway?"

"I never thought about that. I like that idea," Katy said.

"It would be easier to hook up to water and the septic system," Father Williamson said.

"All right, that is where the cottage will be built," Dave said. "You will want to build a garage for your car too."

"You can grow your own flowers anywhere you like," Katy said. "You could set large pots with plants throughout the area also."

"We have some large landscaping rocks being delivered to the Garden and Landscape Store soon, which would look nice to make a flower garden," Dave said. "We will share the vegetable garden at the back of our house. There is no reason to have two vegetable gardens when one large vegetable garden would give an overabundance of food for all of us."

"I like all these ideas," Mother Williamson said. "We sure have a lot to look forward to."

"I have a book of home designs in the house," Dave said. "Let's go to the enclosed porch and take a look at them together."

"When you are ready to sell your home in Oklahoma City, you may store anything you want to keep on the third story of our home," Katy said.

"We have that pavilion at the end of the tunnel that can be used for items to be stored too," Dave said. "I just came up with a great idea. Mother and Father can live in the pavilion."

Everyone laughed and said together, "I don't think so, Dave!" Dave instantly laughed with them.

Katy and Mother Williamson walked up the front porch steps and through the front door. The phone was ringing in the sitting room. "Hello, the Middletons. This is Katy."

"Hi, Katy, this is Sheriff Jesse. Is Dave free to come to the phone?" Sheriff Jesse asked.

"Yes, I will let him know you would like to talk to him," Katy said. "Dave, Sheriff Jesse is on the phone and would like to talk to you!" Katy shouted from the front porch.

"I am coming," Dave said as he hurried up the steps and walked to the sitting room. "Hi, Sheriff Jesse," Dave said, trying to catch his breath from hurrying so fast.

"Dave, we caught those two men taking a baby bunny from a trap they had set in the meadow beside Cedar River," Sheriff Jesse said.

"Really!" Dave exclaimed. "So there must be more than one trap."

"Yes, we found traps set on the banks all along Cedar River," Sheriff Jesse said. "These two men, Mac and Roni, have been very busy making a good amount of money selling what they caught in those traps."

"Who were they selling to?" Dave asked.

"Anyone who sold fish, mice, rabbits, snakes as pets," Sheriff Jesse answered.

"Scott told me he purchased a large goldfish from two men while Katy and I were away for a week in Oklahoma City," Dave said. "We call him Bubbles."

"That goldfish probably came from Cedar River," Sheriff Jesse said.

"Do you want us to put Bubbles back in the river?" Dave asked. "I don't want to be involved in anything illegal."

"No, if Bubbles is happy and content at your house, it is best he stays there," Sheriff Jesse said.

"What will happen to Mac and Roni?" Dave asked.

"As you recall, these two men stole money from Hank's Quick Shop in Springville during the month of February also," Sheriff Jesse said. "There were other convenience stores in the state of Oklahoma they stole money from. Mac and Roni will probably be paying a large fine, doing jail time, and doing community service. We are thinking about removing that stone cottage from Dark Woods. It will be a temptation to someone to use it, and it isn't the safest to live in."

"That is probably a good idea," Dave said. "With that stone cottage gone, we wouldn't have to worry about anyone finding out about our pavilion on the other side of Cedar River."

"I agree," Sheriff Jesse said. "I will keep in touch, and have a good day."

"You too, Sheriff," Dave said as he hung the receiver on the phone base.

"What did Sheriff Jesse want?" Katy asked. "They caught the two men, Mac and Roni, emptying over twenty-five traps along the bank of Cedar River," Dave said.

"It sure would have been easier for Mac and Roni to make a decision to find a good job and earn their money honestly," Father Williamson said.

"I agree, Dad," Dave said. "The time spent setting those traps, checking those traps, hoping they could sell what they caught in those traps seems useless to me. Sheriff Jesse said Mac and Roni have also been charged for robberies at convenience stores throughout the state of Oklahoma."

"Yes, they were the two men who robbed money from Hank's Quick Shop," Katy said. "That was the morning when a bullet from their gun ricocheted from a shelf and landed in Dave's chest."

"Oh my!" Mother Williamson exclaimed. "Mac and Roni have made very poor choices to make a living for themselves."

"They could have had a daily eight-hour job, received a good check, and returned home and relaxed every night," Father Williamson said. "Now they have a large fine to pay, court and attorney costs, perhaps jail time, and do community service with no paycheck."

"I hope they will be able to turn their life around and find a job they like and never think of doing anything like this again," Mother Williamson said. "All of us must remember to pray for Mac and Roni so they will be given a chance to do better things during their journey on the earth that was created by our heavenly Father, God."

"Anybody hungry for a new dessert?" Katy asked.

"Sure!" Dave, Mother, and Father Williamson exclaimed.

"Come to the kitchen, and I will show you what I made," Katy said. She brought out a large pan from the refrigerator.

"It looks delicious. What is it?" Mother Williamson asked.

"It is called 'éclair dessert,'" Katy said. "It is exactly like the éclairs you can purchase in Miss Emily's bakery. Only it is in dessert form."

"It is delicious," Dave said. "May I have a glass of cold milk with mine?" Dave asked.

"Make that two," Father Williamson said.

"Make that three," Mother Williamson added.

"Why don't I make that four!" Katy exclaimed as she carried a tray with four glasses of cold white milk in them.

"You should enter this dessert in the baking contest at the Springville Fair this coming August," Dave suggested.

"I just might do that," Katy said. "Mother, you are welcome to enter baked goods too."

"I will give it some thought," Mother Williamson said as she took another bite of the delicious éclair dessert. "I definitely want this recipe. The ladies at our church in Oklahoma City won't believe it until they taste it."

Chapter 38

"Today is our big day, Katy," Dave said. "What time did Evelyn say we should be at the hospital to pick up Kyle James and Kylie Sue?" he asked.

"Ten o'clock this morning," Katy said.

"We will leave at nine o'clock," Dave said. "That will give us plenty of time to get there. The work traffic will have slowed down by then."

"Father and I will stay at the house with Chester, Samson, and Bubbles," Mother Williamson said. "We will be waiting with great excitement for your return to your home with your son, Kyle James, and daughter, Kylie Sue."

As Dave and Katy walked out of the house to their SUV, Chester ran out the door toward the tall oak trees east of the house.

I have to go back to that stone cottage. Those two men have been caught, so now is my chance to see what is inside. I have to make sure there aren't any cages with animals inside of them. Those animals will not survive if they don't have food, Chester thought as he scampered through the trees and started down the path. He walked over the bridge that crossed over Cedar River. Following the path to his left, he came upon the stone cottage. He walked quietly up to the door and began lifting the lever up and down until the door slightly opened. He pushed on the door, and there standing in front of him was Calli Crow.

"Well, hello there, stranger," Calli Crow said. "I know you. We met by the bushes. You were looking for butterflies. I sure am glad to see you!" Calli Crow exclaimed.

"You are free to go, Calli Crow. Your two owners won't be coming back. They have been arrested by Sheriff Jesse and Deputy James for capturing animals and fish in traps and selling them illegally for money," Chester said.

"What about this?" Calli Crow asked, flying to a large cloth bag lying in the corner of the stone cottage. Chester walked over to the cloth bag and opened it with his sharp claws. As he looked inside the cloth bag, he stepped back immediately.

"I would always see my owners with some of these," Calli Crow said as she used her beak to peck at a twenty-dollar bill.

"I will take ten of these paper bills back to my home," Chester said.

"Isn't that stealing, Chester?" Calli Crow asked.

"It already is stolen money. I want my owners to know about this so they will follow me to this stone cottage, and they can take it to our home and report it to Sheriff Jesse," Chester said.

"How are you going to tell them all this?" Calli Crow asked. "You can't speak their language, and I don't speak their language either."

"Well, that's the thing, Calli Crow. I have a buddy who is a cockatoo. His name is Samson. I will tell him everything, and he will repeat it to my owners. He can speak their language," Chester said.

"May I follow you home, Chester?" Calli Crow asked. "I would like to meet this friend of yours."

"Sure, there are tall oak trees on the east side of my home, which would be a great and safe place for you to stay. It will be great having you as a friend. You and Samson would have a great time talking together," Chester said.

"Thanks, Chester. Let me help you carry a couple of those paper bills," Calli Crow said as she swooped down and picked up two of the paper bills in her beak. "Show the way, Chester!" Calli Crow exclaimed.

"Follow me, Calli Crow," Chester said.

Chester walked up the back porch steps and tapped on the door.

"Hello, Chester, come on in," Mother Williamson said as she opened the door.

"What do you have in your mouth?" Father Williamson asked, watching Chester walk inside the enclosed porch.

"Where did you get this money, Chester?" Mother Williamson asked.

Chester walked to the back door and put his right paw up and stared.

"I think he wants us to follow him," Father Williamson said.

At that very moment, Samson came walking onto the enclosed porch.

"Samson, my good buddy, tell Grampy and Grammy I found these paper bills at the stone cottage in Dark Woods. Also, tell them there are more paper bills in a large bag at the stone cottage," Chester said.

"Stone cottage! Stone cottage! Dark woods! Got to go! Hurry! Hurry!" Samson said loudly.

"We can't leave. I promised Dave and Katy we would be here when they arrive with Kyle and Kylie," Mother Williamson said.

"You stay here. I am going to follow Chester to that stone cottage in Dark Woods," Father Williamson said. "I shouldn't be gone no more than a couple of hours."

"Be careful, John. Take some water with you," Mother Williamson said. "You have no idea how long you will be walking through Dark Woods."

"Thanks," Father Williamson said, giving her a kiss on the cheek.

An hour had passed as Father Williamson and Chester walked over the bridge across Cedar River. Within another hour, they came upon the stone cottage. Father Williamson and Chester walked inside.

"Oh my, this is a lot of money!" Father Williamson exclaimed. "This is going to be too heavy for me to carry back to the house. Look, there is a motorboat tied to a dock. You and I will get in that motorboat with this cloth bag of money. Just on the other side of Cedar River is a pavilion that belongs to Dave and Katy. I know how to let that pressure-treated pine wall down. We can put the cloth bag

of money inside the pavilion where it will be safe until Sheriff Jesse can come."

Chester jumped in the motorboat while Father Williamson untied the rope from the dock.

I remember a motorboat similar to this boat. It was on Halloween night last year. Two boys were in the boat, and I sent Rosco Rat, Ralphie Rat, Sammy Snake, Sissy Snake, Sally Spider, Sonny Spider, Billy Beaver, and Beulah Beaver to stop those boys from getting that enormous robot creature back on its feet that was scaring everyone in Dark Woods, Chester thought.

They reached the entrance of the pavilion. Father Williamson tied the rope of the motor boat to a nearby tree. He jumped out of the boat and stepped onto the ledge between the pressure-treated pine wall and glass doors. He then reached toward the top of the pavilion and removed the two hooks from the heavy bar. Chester was very impressed as he saw his grampy turn the crank on the left side of the pavilion, which made the chain loosen. He then turned the crank on the right side of the pavilion, which slowly lowered the pressure-treated pine wall and let it splash on top of the water. Chester jumped out of the motorboat onto the pressure-treated pine wall and ran through the glass doors that Father Williamson had slid open.

"There, we will hide it in the corner here where it won't be seen by anyone," Father Williamson said. "Let's go, Chester." Chester jumped back in the motorboat while Father Williamson closed the black curtain and slid the glass doors shut. He then started to turn the cranks which lifted the pressure-treated pine wall back in place, covering the entrance to the pavilion. He attached the two hooks to the heavy metal bar on top of the pavilion. Father Williamson slowly walked onto the ledge and made his way through the water of Cedar River and hoisted himself back in the motorboat. Father Williamson pushed the lever of the motorboat to high speed. "Okay, Chester, I will tie this motorboat back to the dock, and we can be on our way back to the house and call Sheriff Jesse," Father Williamson said.

*****

Dave and Katy arrived at the front desk of the Methodist Hospital in Springville, Oklahoma, at ten o'clock.

"Good to see you," Evelyn, the caseworker, said. "A nurse will be waiting for you at the nurse's station to give you instructions on how to care for Kyle James and Kylie Sue and the formula milk they are drinking. You will want to keep them on the formula milk until your family doctor says they may begin drinking regular milk. Every baby is different, so be sure to ask your family doctor about this. The hospital sends a case of formula milk and a supply of items you will need for each baby as a gift."

"That is thoughtful of the hospital," Katy said.

"I am sure it will come in handy," Dave said.

"If you have any questions, don't be afraid to ask," Evelyn said. "The nurses are very helpful at Methodist Hospital and want everything to go smoothly for new parents and children going to their new homes."

Dave, sitting in a wheelchair, held Kyle James in his arms and Katy, sitting in a wheelchair, held Kylie Sue in her arms. Two nurses pushed the wheelchairs to the SUV, which was standing outside the front entrance doors of the hospital. Evelyn, the caseworker, pushed a cart holding the baby supplies and cases of the formula milk the hospital was sending home with Dave and Katy. The nurses helped Dave and Katy place Kyle James and Kylie Sue in their car seats. Dave and Katy thanked everyone and said their goodbyes. Kyle and Kylie slept the entire trip to their new home.

It was one o'clock in the afternoon when Father Williamson and Chester walked through the door of the back porch.

"You are just in time!" Mother Williamson said. "Dave and Katy just drove up."

Mother and Father Williamson were waiting anxiously at the door of the front porch as Dave and Katy got out of the SUV. Dave carried Kyle James in his arms, and Katy carried Kylie Sue in her arms into the house. They placed each baby in a cradle that Father Williamson had made.

"Father sure did a fantastic job making the cradles," Katy said.

"He sure did," Dave said. "While he was working on them at the Garden and Landscape Store, I would peek in now and then. He would always be humming a tune while he worked. I could tell he was enjoying every minute while making these cradles."

"While they are sleeping, let's have lunch," Mother Williamson said. "I made tuna salad sandwiches. I also made a tray of sliced tomatoes, dill pickles, and lettuce that you can put on your sandwiches if you like."

"Don't forget the potato chips," Father Williamson said.

"What's for dessert?" Dave asked.

"I made a new dessert," Mother Williamson said. "It is called a strawberry supreme dessert."

"Another new recipe, Mother," Katy said.

"Yes, and if you like it, you may add it to your recipe book," Mother Williamson answered.

"I have something to share with you," Father Williamson said. "Chester did that right paw thing again while you were at the hospital this morning. He must have talked to Samson because Samson let us know the money Chester had in his mouth came from the stone cottage in Dark Woods. I followed him, and he led me to that stone cottage on the other side of Cedar River. We went inside, and you aren't going to believe what I found."

"What?" Dave asked.

"A large cloth bag full of money," Father Williamson answered.

"Where is it?" Dave asked.

"Chester and I couldn't carry it because it was very heavy, so we got in this motorboat and speedily crossed Cedar River to your pavilion. We placed it in a dark corner inside the pavilion. I thought you and I could go down and walk through that tunnel and get that cloth bag of money and bring it up where we can keep an eye on it till Sheriff Jesse can come."

"That sounds like a good idea, Dad," Dave said. "I will get the spotlight from the bedroom."

Dave and Father Williamson began their journey through the dark, cold tunnel that led to the open room of the pavilion. As they entered the room, they heard voices outside.

"Who is on the other side of that wall?" Dave whispered.

"I don't know, but I think we will soon be finding out," Father Williamson whispered back. "Stand over here in this dark corner, and stay quiet." Dave and Father Williamson stood quietly as the pressure-treated pine wall was lowered and splashed in the water. The glass doors were slid open, and the black curtains were pushed to one side. Two teenage boys walked inside.

"What are your names?" Dave asked as he and Father Williamson stepped away from the dark corner.

"My name is Mitch," said the tall thin teenage boy.

"My name is Dan," said the short stocky-built teenage boy.

"I know you, boys," Dave said. "You are the boys who maneuvered a large robot through Dark Woods to scare everyone on Halloween night a year ago." Dan and Mitch instantly put their heads down. "What are you doing here?" Dave asked.

"We were hired by Mac and Roni to help empty traps along Cedar River," Mitch said.

"Don't you know that it is illegal to set traps in Dark Woods and Cedar River?" Dave asked. "You are also trespassing on my property."

"We wanted to earn some money. That's all," Dan said.

"You won't be working for Mac and Roni any longer," Father Williamson said. "They are sitting in a jail cell this very minute."

"You both are coming with me," Dave said. "We will be turning you over to Sheriff Jesse." Dave closed the cloth bag of money and tied it with the rope that was attached to it. "You boys will be carrying this for me as we walk through that tunnel," Dave said. "Follow me, and don't get any ideas of trying to get away because my partner is right behind you."

The stocky-built teenage boy, Dan, took one end of the cloth bag, and the tall thin teenage boy, Mitch, took hold of the other end of the cloth bag.

"This is really heavy. What do you have in here, a dead body?" the stocky-built teenage boy, Dan, asked.

"Be quiet and start walking," Dave said.

They reached the end of the tunnel and walked through the room that led to the creaky steps of the staircase. After walking up the steep staircase, they walked through the bookcase opening and saw Mother Williamson and Katy feeding Kyle James and Kylie Sue a bottle of their formula while sitting calmly in the upholstered wing-back rocking chairs.

"Shshsh!" Katy said. "They are almost asleep."

"Who is that, and what are they carrying?" Mother Williamson asked with a shocked look on her face.

"We will explain later," Father Williamson answered. "Meet us in the sitting room after you lay the children in their cradles."

Dave immediately called Sheriff Jesse and let him know about the cloth bag of money that was found in the stone cottage and also the two teenage boys, Dan and Mitch, trespassing on his property. Sheriff Jesse and Deputy James came immediately and were over-joyed that Father Williamson and Chester had found a cloth bag full of money in the stone cottage.

"This is probably money that was stolen from many stores around Oklahoma by Mac and Roni," Deputy James said. "This will be used as evidence against them in a court of law."

"Don't forget these ten paper bills," Father Williamson said as he handed Sheriff Jesse the paper bills, which amounted to two hundred dollars. "Chester found the cloth bag of money first and came back to the house with these paper bills in his mouth."

"Thank you for your help, Chester, and your honesty, John," Sheriff Jesse said as he took the fifty dollars from Father Williamson and placed it in the cloth bag.

"What do you plan to do with these two teenage boys, Mitch and Dan?" Dave asked.

"They will be taken to the Springfield, Oklahoma, Police Department," Sheriff Jesse said. "We will call their parents and let them know the boys will have to show up for juvenile court and explain why they were trespassing on your property," Sheriff Jesse said. "I will keep you informed."

"Thanks, Sheriff Jesse," Dave said.

"Yes, thank you," Father Williamson replied.

"Where is Chester?" Sheriff Jesse asked. "I want to give him a big thanks for all his help in this."

"Chester!" Dave shouted. "He usually comes when his name is called. Follow me. Let's go see where he has gone too."

Everyone walked into the room that was made into a nursery. There curled up on the carpet under Kyle James's cradle was Chester, and standing under Kylie Sue's cradle was Samson, fast asleep.

"Well, I will thank Chester another time," Sheriff Jesse whispered. "I will give you a call when I can tell you more about that cloth bag of money and what those two teenage boys have to say."

"I'll have something good for you to eat when you stop by," Katy said.

"Your baby boy and baby girl are beautiful," Sheriff Jesse remarked. "I am happy for both of you. I will be on my way."

"Keep in touch, and thanks again," Mother and Father Williamson said as they shook Sheriff Jesse's hand. Deputy James had already escorted the two teenage boys, Mitch and Dan, to the squad car. Sheriff Jesse drove them to the Springville, Oklahoma, Police Department.

"Dad, you and I need to go back through that tunnel and bring that pressure-treated pine wall up and hook it to the top of the pavilion," Dave said.

"That's right. We sure don't need any other intruders sneaking in that pavilion," Father Williamson said. "Let's get it done right now so we can lock both those doors down there and get this bookcase closed for the night."

"We will be waiting for you when you get back," Mother Williamson said. "We need to make a schedule of who stays in the nursery for the first night feeding and who gets to sleep."

"Dave and I will take care of the first night feeding," Katy said. "Set your alarm clock for three o'clock in the morning. That will be close to their next feeding."

"We will do that," Mother Williamson said in a kind voice.

"This definitely is a precious moment in our lives," Katy said as she watched their children sleep soundly in their cradles and Chester and Samson sleeping on the carpet beneath their cradles. "I can't think of anything more precious than our two children, Kyle James and Kylie Sue."

"We can't forget Chester, our Maine coon cat, Samson, our cockatoo, and Bubbles, our goldfish," Dave said.

"I would never forget them, Dave," Katy remarked in a kind voice. "We have so much to look forward to."

"Yes, we do, and I am glad Mother and Father Williamson will be able to share every moment and all the good times in the future days with us," Dave said.

About the Author

J. Eileen finished writing her third book, *A Precious Moment*, in the year 2022. It is a sequel to her first book, *A Dream Comes True*, and her second book, *When It's Right, It's Right*.

J. Eileen's books offer the readers what their life could be like no matter what tragedy, sadness, or any disappointing experience or type of displeasure they may have because of the nonfulfillment of one's hopes or expectations they have faced in the past. She wants to inspire the reader to build castles of possibilities within their life's journey as she was inspired to become an author.

J. Eileen was raised on a farm in central Iowa, where there were many animals to care for. As a child, during the summer months, she would go to the creek in the back pasture with her dog, Lassie, and her cat, Priscilla. Her mother would let her take a snack consisting of peanut butter and jelly sandwiches and home-baked chocolate chip cookies. As the dairy cows grazed, Lassie and Priscilla would sit beside her along the creek with clear, cool water running through it. She would sing songs to her Savior, Jesus Christ, and share some of her sandwiches and cookies with Lassie and Priscilla.

As she has resided on an acreage since the year 1989, a cat now and then would show up on her porch, needing food and care. During the month of October in the year 2016, a long-haired cat was sitting at the end of her porch at three o'clock in the morning. She opened her garage door, and the cat ran inside giving no thought or urge to leave. It was as if the cat were saying, "I'm here to stay!" She fed him, and he made himself at home immediately. He loved to be combed and brushed but did not like his large white paws touched. On his forehead was brown hair forming the letter M. Doing research on the Internet, she found he was a Maine coon cat. She named him "Chester." He always came when she called his name. They went on walks together throughout her four-acre property. Chester also loved to go for rides in the SUV as long as J. Eileen was driving. As three years have passed, Chester will now let J. Eileen touch his paws as he lays curled up on her lap while being rocked in the teak rocking chair that sits on her porch.

To this day, they are best of friends and respect each other in every way. J. Eileen often wondered what all the animals' stories would be that she cared for if they could talk.

Her fourth book will have the title *Memories*. It is a sequel to her first book, *A Dream Comes True*; her second book, *When It's Right, It's Right*; and her third book, *A Precious Moment*.

About the Illustrator

Alexa Yoakum was raised in a small town in central Iowa with her family and pets. At a very young age, she found her love of art. During her free time, Alexa Yoakum would draw animals, people, and even scenery. Her passion for drawing grew, and the need for sketchbooks also grew! Her family supported her love for art, and every birthday and Christmas, she received a sketchbook.

When Alexa Yoakum was in elementary school, one of her art pieces was picked and placed in an artist's collection. In high school, Alexa Yoakum learned different techniques and mediums to expand her love of art. Alexa Yoakum loved learning the different medium styles: pottery, mixed media, painting, and drawing. Her favorite type of art is glass etching, watercolor markers, and drawing with graphite or colored pencils.

"I love drawing animals and using my color pencils to bring them to life! I have done portraits of animals as they are my inspiration for art. I would like to inspire people to use art to express themselves and bring their ideas to life!" She loves bringing ideas to life and sharing her art to bring joy to people!

Ingram Content Group UK Ltd.
Milton Keynes UK
UKHW020433310323
419423UK00001B/9